Th

By Felicity Rose

Edited by Nicola Lovick

To my husband who always believes in me and banishes my doubts.
I love you always.

Chapter 1

My heart was hammering against my ribcage, my throat was dry and my chest was tight.

My feet pounded against the pavement as I ran.

Quickly glancing over my shoulder, I could see he was gaining on me.

I had to keep going.

I think he was shouting something, but the noise in my ears blocked it out.

I kept running as fast as my legs would carry me, all the way up to my front door.

I bent over to catch my breath, the blood rushing to my head.

I stood up and steadied myself, pulling the ear buds out of my ears.

'I think you're getting slower,' I said, regaining my posture.

He had given up running and was stumbling up to the front door, wheezing as he went.

'Jeez, Saskia,' he panted. 'When did you get so damn fast?'

'I didn't!' I laughed. 'You're just getting old.'

I ruffled Matt's hair as he bent over, still struggling to breathe.

'Race you!' I said, skipping into the house, leaving my housemate at the door.

He stood shaking his head, then ambled in behind me.

I ran straight up the stairs and into the bathroom.

Peeling off my sweaty leggings, top and underwear, I got into the shower and pressed the On button, stepping out of the way to let the cold water warm up.

Wrapped in my towel, I wandered across the landing to my bedroom.

'I'm making coffee and crumpets, Sass, do you want any?' Matt shouted upstairs.

'Yes please!' I yelled back.

I pulled on my favourite light jeans and a classic white tee and blow-dried my long, straight hair, checking my reflection in the mirror before going downstairs.

Matt was at the kitchen table, already starting on his crumpets.

'Thank you!' I chirped, sitting across from him in front of my own plate and mug.

'You recovered yet, old man?' I asked, between mouthfuls of fluffy, buttery crumpet.

'Saskia,' he said, looking serious. 'I will get better. And I will beat you!'

'Uh-huh, sure.' I grinned at him as he stood up from the table.

He smiled back at me and put his plate in the sink.

'Right, I'm off for a shower, see you in a bit.'

I sat at the table, alone with my coffee.

There's no better feeling than the first lovely sunny mornings of the year.

It still wasn't clement enough to sit outside, but I was

basking in the warmth of the sunshine pouring through the French doors, creating little dust motes that danced around in the air.

Although fairly small, the table seated four people comfortably and pulled out to accommodate a further four on emergency chairs when needed.

A dark-red cloth covered it and a small wooden bowl sat in the centre with a few apples in it.

It wasn't the biggest house; a three-bed mid-terrace with a quaint but overlooked back garden.

Myself and my housemates had lovingly put our stamp on it and I loved its contemporary feel.

The early morning birds were singing to each other as they flew from branch to branch in the magnolia tree that was starting to bloom outside the back door.

Every year we cut it back, tidying it up but making it look a little sad through the winter. Then, as soon as the warming spring air hit, it would slowly wake up until summer arrived, bringing with it the most beautiful pink blossom with a scent that crept into the kitchen whenever the doors were open.

I peered into the bottom of my mug to find all the golden liquid gone. I frowned at its emptiness, knowing that was my cue to leave.

Wandering into the front room I tried to remember where I had dumped my bag and coat last night. I scanned the room, noticing the curtains were still closed. I pulled at the heavy grey material and dust flew off them as the light poured in.

The room was an odd shape which would have been difficult to furnish, but Matt had a good friend who had made us bespoke furniture for a fraction of the price it would normally cost.

Heavy wooden bookshelves filled three of the walls. They were at bursting point, yet still we found space for more books.

The shelves needed dusting again, I noticed as the sunlight hit them, specks of dust blew around the room like tiny fairies dancing in the sun.

It didn't matter how much you dusted; it would gather again and again, along with the little knick-knacks and life clutter that didn't have any other home.

Snowy – the cat that belonged to Matt – gave me daggers for waking him, then got up and stretched before running out the door, tripping me up as he went.

Snowy was a little grumpy to anyone that wasn't Matt, but on nights when it was just me and him, he would sit on my lap purring like a train and drooling on my legs.

When I had asked Matt why he would call a black cat Snowy, he laughed and told me that was exactly why.

I failed to understand his logic, but secretly quite liked the little furball.

I located my jacket and bag. Unfortunately, Snowy had been keeping my coat warm for me.

It was a little creased and covered in cat hair, but I was going to be late so I gave it a shake, brushing off the worst of the fluff, pulled it on, picked up my bag and headed to the front door, tripping over Snowy again on the way out.

I put my ear buds in, tapped Shuffle on Spotify and started my walk to work to the sound of Alicia Keys.

I unlocked the door of my little bookshop.

First thing in the morning was my favourite part of the day. The smell of the books was at its strongest when I first walked through the door after a long night.

I'd opened Just One More Chapter three years ago and had loved every minute.

From a very young age I loved books and was reading before I started school thanks to my terrific mum who shared my love for them.

I ran out of books at primary school and my teachers began to get in high school books to keep me challenged. From there, my passion grew. I would read anything I could get my hands on, from Jayne Eyre to my dad's Haynes manuals, though I always favoured fiction.

Being able to drift off to experience other worlds in my imagination was the best part. I would read between two and four books a week, spending every spare minute I had with my nose in one.

One day at school, we each had a session with a career adviser. She asked me what I wanted to do when I was a grown up. I hadn't given it much thought as I was still quite young, so told her I didn't know, feeling a little ashamed.

The kind lady had smiled at me, telling me it was fine to not know and that the best place to start was working out what I enjoyed.

'Well that's easy,' I replied. 'Books! Books are my passion!' And it was at that moment that I decided what I was going to do with my life.

Once my school years were over, I was still sure about what I wanted to do. I took a job as a waitress. It didn't challenge my brain, but, by keeping a smile on my face and working every hour I could, the tips mounted up quickly enough that I was able to put enough money aside for me to fund my dream.

It had taken a lot of determination, hard work and the support of my fantastic family and friends, but, between us, we managed to find the perfect premises with a-just-about-affordable lease and the real work began.

Mum, Dad and my two closest friends, Beth and Matt, stripped the walls, ripped up carpets, fitted bookshelves and a desk..

When it came to naming the shop, I had gone round in circles, brainstorming but coming up blank, until it finally hit me.

It was Mum who had indirectly come up with the name for the shop. Every night in high school, she would come and tell me it was time for lights out and I would always beg 'Just one more chapter' and it just became our thing.

There could be nothing better suited.

From there, it was setting up a website and social media pages and arranging to have the outside sign made and put up.

Finally, hot and dusty, slightly warm beer in our hands, the five of us stood outside on the pavement and admired the final result. I had poured everything into this and none of it would have been possible without the help of my friends and family.

I often recalled those early days as I walked round my shop each morning, running my fingers over the shelves and straightening each book to perfection.

It was quite a light and spacious shop with shelves all around the walls, only stopping to allow a door out to the back where I kept any spare stock next to a small toilet and kitchen.

My desk, complete with till and laptop, was near the door so I was able to greet my customers as they came in.

I had wanted a snug feel, so had positioned more bookcases in the middle of the shop, creating makeshift booths with comfy chairs. It made it cosier and invited people to spend more time making their decisions.

Located in a coastal town, it had a lovely community feel. The kettle was always on and I knew all my regulars by name.

The morning went quickly; sorting and cleaning in between serving a handful of customers. My stomach was rumbling; it must be lunchtime already.

The sun was still shining as I put the 'back in 10' sign on the door and walked round the corner to the little deli, the queue spilling out onto the street as it always was.

The food was second to none and prepared fresh while you waited.

I spotted the guy at the counter; rushed off his feet and looking less-than-ecstatic, as usual.

Having attempted small talk with him over the years I had been eating there, I had found out that he owned the place and worked it all on his own.

He was a man of very few words and always seemed far too distracted to talk, but, my, he was beautiful.

It was tiny, with a counter running across the end, separating the customers from the kitchen.

The sandwich fillings were on display behind the glass in chillers, making the decision tough for anyone.

Being a creature of habit, in all the years I had been getting my lunch there, I had only tried a few things but always gone back to my usual.

Pesto chicken and cheese salad with half a brown baguette.

Salad Guy – as I had dubbed him – nodded at me as he rang up the total on the till.

I watched him moving around, preparing my salad.

Beautifully toned arms showed under his short sleeves and where his apron was tied around his waist, I could just make out the outline of his pecs.

And when he turned around...that arse! I was lost in a daydream when he turned back, holding out my bag of food, catching me staring wistfully at him. Blushing slightly, I took the bag and thanked him, catching his eye for a little longer than needed. He mumbled and tore his gaze away quickly, but his face also started to colour slightly. I could swear he was almost smiling.

The warmer weather was bringing out the holiday-makers and, luckily for me, they all seemed to enjoy a good bookshop browse.

'Good afternoon,' I called to a couple as they wandered in. 'Hello,' the lady said as she smiled. The man nodded at me to acknowledge my greeting.

I would put them in their early forties and could tell instantly that they were both avid readers. They both went straight to a different section, and, as they perused the selection, neither could help themselves but touch the books, lightly running their fingers over the spines as if to connect them with the right book for them.

I let them browse a little longer, then said,

'Are you staying nearby?'

'Yes,' said the man, looking up politely from the book in his hand. 'In the bed and breakfast just up the hill.'

'The rooms are so sweet,' the lady added, walking over to

the till. 'And the view is just breath-taking. Do you live close?'

'Yes, about ten minutes' walk from here. It really is as pretty as a picture.'

Leaving with five books between them, they thanked me and left.

Even after all this time, I still felt a rush each time a book was purchased.

The afternoon was quiet, so once I had updated the shop social media and added a few items to my order list, I opened my latest book and became lost in my other world, reading right to the end. I closed the book and signed deeply. I loved nothing more than becoming immersed in a book, feeling as though I knew the characters personally and got how they felt. But a little bit of sadness always crept in once I had read the last page; left feeling as though I had lost a dear friend.

Before leaving for the night, I made sure everything was switched off and locked up.

As I walked home, I had time to focus on my evening out, thinking of some outfit options. Instead of the female power ballads I'd walked to work with, I went with noughties pop, powering through the ten minutes home with a spring in my step.

I had plenty of time to get ready, so had a lengthy shower and was even able to use a five-minute miracle mask on my hair while I shaved my legs.

Beth had suggested we have a quiet one so we were just going to our local bar, but we took any excuse to dress up.

I made my way to my bedroom, wrapped in my bath towel, with my long, mousey, sun- streaked hair twisted up in a towel. I moisturised head to toe, lying on the bed to dry off.

My phone vibrated on the bedside table. It was Beth, texting to say she would be home in ten with wine.

I heard the front door go and Matt shout, 'Sass, you home?'

I put on my cream fluffy robe. 'Yeah, I'm here!' I yelled back, making Snowy jump off the bed and run downstairs to meet her master.

'Beth and I are going to Fred's, you fancy it?' I called down.

'Thanks, Sass!' He appeared in the open doorway. 'I'm taking Stacey out for dinner tonight, though. He grinned like a Cheshire cat showing his straight white teeth.

'You are so smitten!' I told him, his smile infectious.

'You got me!' He feigned an arrow to his heart and disappeared into his bedroom.

Within ten minutes, Beth was home and Matt was on his way to pick up Stacey.

Beth had been one of my closest friends ever since I could remember.

She and her family lived a few houses up from us from about four years old until her parents sold their house and moved away only a couple of years ago.

We went through school together and told each other all our secrets. Every crush or embarrassing story there was to know, we had already told each other.

When someone notices yesterday's underwear falling from the leg of your two-day-old jeans whilst walking through the corridors in school and grabs them before anyone else sees, you just know they are there for life.

Beth was – as she put it – abnormally tall. It probably didn't help having a friend as short as me, but, at nearly six foot, she was pretty tall for a girl.

She was always bullied at school for being taller than the boys, but pretended it didn't hurt.

I was quite feisty as a child and very protective over my friends, so would often threaten the boys and was pulled into the headmaster's office on more than one occasion for getting into fights with them after hearing them badmouth Beth.

Now in our late twenties, Beth is an absolute beauty.

With shoulder-length dark hair, olive skin and big brown eyes, being tall just adds to Beth's allure.

At just over five feet and with my long mousey hair, fair skin and freckles, I often felt back then that I paled in comparison, but my looks had matured, and although I may not be a tall, dark beauty, I was fond of my porcelain complexion and natural beauty.

'How was the shop today?' Beth asked as she opened the bottle of Pecorino and poured us a glass each. The light, citrusy taste tingled my tastebuds as I savoured the first sip.

'Starting to pick up again,' I answered as I pulled the clothes in Beth's wardrobe from one side to the other, having decided against everything in my own. 'How about you, good day?'

Beth looked gorgeous as always with light-blue jeans and a pretty white top. 'Same shit, different day!' She laughed, reaching past me and grabbing a hot-pink, low-cut camisole top. 'I love this one on you,' she said as she handed it to me.

I wandered into my room and came back in a pink bra and skinny jeans – they were one thing we couldn't share. I pulled the top on and we stood side by side in front of the mirror and both nodded our approval.

We finished the bottle in record time and were both a little merry as we locked the front door behind us.

I tottered out into the street in my stupidly high heels while Beth wore her little kitten heels as she always did so we didn't look like Little and Large on a night out.

We walked past quaint little cottages and up the hill to the bar as the waves crashed against the dark harbour walls. The tide was all the way in, making it impossible to even make out where the sand had been a few hours earlier.

Freddie's Bar was alive with the hum of chatter over the usual eclectic music choice. There was always something for everyone, from cheesy and swinging sixties to rock and roll or heavy metal. If you stayed for more than one drink, there would be something to get you dancing in your seat.

Tonight was a normal Friday night. Plenty of regulars milling around the bar and filling the booths, laughing and winding down ready for the weekend. Plus our fair share of out-of-town troublemakers.

We pushed our way through, Beth leading to part the crowd for me and managing to grab two seats at the bar.

We had been drinking for a few hours and were a little worse for wear when Beth nodded over to the door, whispering, 'Holy Christ, look at him.'

I turned to spot the man Beth had found, but quickly spun back round. 'It's Salad Guy! He runs Pastrami Jim's, the deli I go to for lunch every day!'

It was then that I noticed how much quieter it had become, as people had left the bar to move onto the nightclubs and bars or to go home, leaving just the regulars and a few drunks having a ball on the dance floor.

I slowly turned back around to take another peek. He looked even more beautiful in jeans and a tight black t-shirt, really showing off those pecs I had strained to see that afternoon.
He had walked in with another guy, and they were making their way over to a table to the right of the bar.

I tried to steer the conversation away from him before Beth got the idea to set us up.

'So... How's Benny boy?' I asked in a sing-song tone.

'It just keeps getting better, you know?' Beth gushed.

Beth had been seeing Ben for almost a year.

I had met him a few times, but felt as though I should know him better by now.

I was quite surprised by his appearance when Beth first brought him to meet me and Matt.

Ben was a little shorter than Beth – as a lot of men were – and he had sandy hair that flopped around his face and in his bright-green eyes like long, shaggy fur.

He wasn't an unattractive man, just not the model type you would expect to see on her arm. The love in her eyes as she introduced him told me everything I needed to know, though.

He was a really sweet guy and gave her all she could want or need.

'Ah, if only I did,' I muttered, trying not to let my single streak take away from Beth's happiness.

It had been a while, about eighteen months now, without so much as a sniff of a decent guy.

There had been plenty of fun and flings in my past, most recently a one-night stand with some guy I met on a hen weekend away. I had woken up the next morning, in his hotel room, full of regret and in desperate need of mouthwash.

We had awkwardly exchanged numbers, but he never called and I probably wouldn't have answered if he did.

That was when I decided I was ready for something real. And if it didn't feel real, I would rather be single.

'Go speak to him,' said Beth, breaking the self-pity party in my head.

'Who? Salad Guy? God, no. What would I say?'

Beth rolled her eyes at me. 'You will never find a man if you don't speak to them. And what do you have to lose?'

'Only the best salads in town,' I said, knowing my argument wouldn't hold up.

I looked over to see Salad Guy's friend en route to the toilet.

'Fuck it,' I said. I had sunk two bottles of wine and at least four different cocktails while making my way through the drinks menu. The alcohol was taking hold. 'I'm gonna do it.'

Beth did a little whoop and squeezed my hand as a good-luck gesture.

He looked up at me as I got nearer and I saw that almost smile creep back onto his face.

I started to get a little flustered, but couldn't change direction now; it would be far too obvious and, anyway, I had plenty of Dutch courage, I remembered as I regained my composure.

'Hey, Salad Guy!' I mentally slapped my face and cursed my stupid inability to speak to guys – especially the hot ones.

'Um, hi, Salad Girl,' he said tentatively.

'Sorry, it's because I don't know your name and I have salad at your deli most days, and—'

'James—' He cut me off. 'Jim for short and, yes, I remember you. Nice to have loyal customers.'

I prayed that the next thing out of my mouth would sound far more interesting, intellectual and mature than I had managed so far.

'Jim, as in Pastrami Jim's. That's good!' I laughed, failing miserably and hoping I didn't sound too crazy.

'Yes, that was kind of the idea, uh, Salad Girl.'

'Saskia, my name is Saskia. I run the book store just around the corner from your deli. I mean the one you run, or own. Do you own it?

I closed my mouth as I realised this was one of those moments that my dad had told me about, you know, the ones where you should have already stopped talking but can still hear your own voice.

His face softened and he gave a little laugh. 'Yes, I own it. I must admit that my parents bought it for me when I got out of university, but, yes, I own and run it.'

He shifted slightly in his seat and suddenly I felt as though I had outstayed my welcome.

'Well, it's uh, nice to see you out of the apron,' I muttered, immediately regretting yet another sentence from my mouth.

I glanced up at his handsome face for a moment, and, instead of the pained expression I expected to see, his mouth was turned up at the corner in the start of a grin.

I smiled, then turned away, going back to my seat as quickly as my dangerously high heels would carry me.

Beth stared at me with wide eyes as I sat back at the bar and drained the dregs of my cocktail.

'Well?' she demanded.

'He's – nice. We chatted. His name is Jim.'

'Nice? That's it?'

'Very polite and uninterested, unfortunately,' I said, feeling a little deflated after my sudden bout of confidence and kicking myself for sounding like such an idiot.

'He barely smiled the whole time I spoke to him. He most definitely isn't the real thing. But I don't think I embarrassed myself too much, so can still get away with buying his delish salads.'

'What *is* the real thing?'

I'd thought about this a lot. 'It's that feeling you get when you're with someone, that happiness that they fill you with just by looking at their face, or being in their company. It's not wanting to leave their side, and missing them as soon as you do. It's wanting to wake up every morning next to them and fall asleep in their arms each night. It's—'

'Like a romance novel?' she offered.

'Yes!' Just like a romance novel. 'Ah, how the hell would I know? It's something I've never bloody had!'

I looked over at Beth, hoping for a giggle at my failed love life to cheer me up, but instead found her staring wistfully into the distance, Ben clearly on the brain.

We giggled through the remainder of the night. It was a much-needed catch-up as Beth was rarely home these days. She enjoyed waking up in Ben's bed far too much to come home to me and Matt.

We stumbled into the house at almost 2 a.m. We somehow managed to make cheese on toast and a cup of tea each and took our plates of oozing goodness upstairs.

'Shush, you will wake Matt!' I scolded in a shouty whisper.

'He's out, remember?' Beth loud whispered back. 'He's staying with Stacey.' She closed her lips tight as if she had just revealed a naughty secret.

'Ooooh, Stacey!' I giggled. 'Why you still whispering then?'

We sat on Beth's bedroom floor, surrounded by cushions and blankets like teenagers at a sleepover, eating our toast and watching *Mean Girls*.

Saturday morning started the way Friday night had finished. On Beth's bedroom floor, next to empty plates and mugs.

Snowy had given up waiting to be fed and had helped himself to the hardened drips of cheese from the plates next to my face.

'Shit!' I sat up with a jump, waking Beth. 'What time is it? I need to get to work.'

Beth just groaned and rolled over. I checked my watch and realised that I had only been asleep for a handful of hours and that it was, in fact, only 7 a.m.

I left Beth to sleep in, and went to get ready, my head spinning as I stood up.

After a shower and a coffee, I was feeling surprisingly OK, considering the amount of alcohol we had put away last night.

The walk to work also helped; both the fresh air and the bacon sandwich I picked up from the little bakery on my way in.

I had a student doing work experience with me on Saturdays. Jenny was a lovely girl, and had so much enthusiasm, but she also stopped me from having my usual hangover Saturdays reading a book. I had to be in shop owner mode, teaching her everything I could.

'So how often do you place an order?' Jenny asked as we were going through the ordering process.

'As and when, really. I always keep track of what sells so that I can order as a particular title runs low.'

Jenny nodded, clearly committing the information to memory.

For the remainder of the afternoon, I sat with Jenny as she played around with some marketing campaigns, showing her how to create eye-catching adverts and brainstorming different ideas to find new customers.

I had really grown to like Jenny. She was very sweet and loved to talk. She was a book nerd just like me and we would spend hours discussing our latest read while tidying up and cleaning around the shop.

I was generally very glad of her company as it got lonely through the quiet weeks.

On Sundays the shop was closed, my precious day off.

Waking to the morning sunshine instead of the harsh alarm was reason enough for it to be precious.

I stretched and yawned, smiling as I let the day off feeling wash over me.

I lay in bed, scrolling through my social media pages for a while before dragging myself out of bed.

I cleaned my teeth and pulled on my gym kit, summoning the motivation to drag my arse to the gym.

I had always looked after my body and was pretty proud of my lean physique. Being in my early twenties, I was lucky enough to be able to eat what I wanted without too much worry about weight gain, but also worked out every chance I got to help maintain it.

I spent half an hour on the treadmill, alternating between a fast walk and a run, then managed some abs on the mat. After an hour, I told myself I had earned some time in the sauna.

As I sat there, my mind wandered to the romance novel I was currently engrossed in. I had only started it yesterday, but was already halfway through and didn't want it to end. I wondered if the men from these books actually existed, then reprimanded myself for nearly breaking the magic. Of course they existed, I just needed to find mine.

Chapter 2

When Monday rolled around again, I found myself wandering to Pastrami Jim's for my lunchtime salad.

I had been over the awkward conversation in my head a thousand times, every time cringing at how embarrassing it had been. Yet still, I couldn't help the excitement building about seeing him again.

There was a tall blonde at the front of the counter, flirting shamelessly with Jim. She giggled and touched her face constantly and even flicked her long, bleached hair in the face of the guy behind her a few times, making him tut and step back.

Jim appeared to be enjoying the attention and gave her a smile as he handed over her food. She flicked her hair once more then turned around, wiggling her butt all the way out.

I watched Jim's smiling expression change as soon as her back turned, and even caught a slight eye roll as she walked away. I wondered if he did the same to me.

As I got to the counter, he looked up at me, catching me off guard by looking even more beautiful close up.

'Hi, Saskia, you want your usual?'

I looked up at that gorgeous face, his dark hair and stubble adding to his good looks.

'Hey, Jim,' I said as casually as I could, but noticed

something was different. He was smiling – at me. A full-on smile that even reached his eyes. Not like the forced smile blondie had received.

'It's a lovely day today, isn't it?'

'Yes, the holiday season is upon us,' I replied, wondering why I had suddenly started talking like my nan.

He smiled at my awkwardness, 'It's the best thing for business around here.'

'Yes, it gets very quiet when the holiday-makers go.'

Feeling quite proud that I had uttered a full sentence without sounding like a complete idiot, or an eighty year old, I realised that we were both staring at each other, and the queue behind me was starting to grow.

'Ahem,' the lady directly behind me cleared her throat loudly, bringing me crashing back down to earth.

Feeling a little uncomfortable, I paid and thanked him, turning and bumping into the lady and muttering apologies on the way out.

I placed my food on the counter and went back to the kitchen to make a cup of tea. As the kettle boiled, I re-ran the embarrassing moment in the deli, but rather than dwelling on the rude lady, I analysed Jim's behaviour; he was very friendly today. I felt a little hope flutter around my chest. I sat back at the counter and took my lunch out of the bag. The receipt dropped out and there was another piece of paper folded with it.

Dear Saskia,

I hope you don't find this too forward, but I would love to take you out for a drink.

Here is my number.
I hope to hear from you soon.
Salad Guy

I read and re-read the note until it started to sink in. Maybe he *was* interested. But so bloody polite.
I snapped a picture of the note and sent it to Beth with the caption:

Got a little extra with my salad today.

Her immediate response was:

If you don't do this, you are banned from ever whinging about being single again!

I somehow managed to wait until the end of the day to contact Jim. Trying my hardest to play it cool.

By the time I typed out the message, I was back home, in my PJs, waiting for my lasagne to cook.

I wrote four different messages before deciding to go with simplicity, hit Send, then closed my eyes, as if it would help the response.

Hi Jim,
I would like that very much.
Saskia

I had finished my tea by the time his response came through.

Great! Are you free Saturday night?

I gave an excited squeal, making Snowy jump off his

radiator bed and eye me sulkily as he walked away.

We confirmed the arrangements and I texted Beth to tell her the good news.

When I opened up my emails on Wednesday morning, there was an email from a publishing company in my inbox. There was an author who wanted to do a book signing in my shop next week.

She was a very well-known author; this would be fantastic for business.

I called the number on the letter before I had even taken off my jacket, perching on the edge of the stool behind the till, bag still hanging at my side.

It rang once or twice before a lady answered.

'Good morning, Golden Publishing, how may I help?' came the slightly plummy voice down the telephone.

'Oh hello there, Saskia Matthews speaking. You sent me an email to say that Emily Trevor would like to attend a book signing at my book shop.'

Just about keeping my cool, I fidgeted with excitement.

'Ah, yes, Just One More Chapter,' the lady confirmed.

We set a date and I thanked Sylvia for her help, feeling as though I owed her a great gratitude just for answering the phone and making this happen.

The book signing, although very exciting, did nothing to take my mind off Jim and by the time Friday arrived, I was filled with so much anticipation I thought I might burst when he touched my hand as he gave me my salad and said,

'I'm looking forward to tomorrow.'All I could muster was a nervous giggle and a smile.

Saturday went at a snail's pace and my clock-watching did nothing to help. Jenny had called in the morning to tell me she wasn't well, so I told her not to worry and to rest up, but now I had no one to help pass the time.

The shop was quiet too. As if it was trying to torture me with its silence and the longest day possible.

My excitement was mixed with nerves about my first date with Jim.

I worried about my awkwardness and if it would alter any attraction he may have for me.

The problem was, the more I tried to act normally, the more awkward I became. It was like watching a cringey comedy half hiding behind a cushion, except there was no cushion to hide behind, and I was playing the lead role.

By the time I was locking up the shop, I had gone from being nervous enough to cancel, back to letting the excitement take hold.

Beth was waiting at the kitchen table with a glass of wine for me when I arrived home on Saturday evening.

Once I had showered, Beth appeared in the doorway ready to help with my outfit.

'What about these?' she asked as she pulled my dark-blue skinny jeans out of the wardrobe and held them up.

'Yes, OK,' I said, nodding my approval. 'What top, though?'

I stood back and scanned through my wardrobe until my gaze settled on one of my favourite tops.

'How about this?' I asked, pulling out a pale mint-green dressy, shoestring vest top.

'Let's see!' she ordered.

I pulled it over my head and turned to face her as I smoothed the sides down.

'Perfect!' she said, clapping her hands together.

I completed the outfit with my silver strappy heels and stood back to check my reflection. The jeans hugged my small frame and the top was just low enough for a bit of cleavage. I was hoping it gave the right impression; whatever that was.

I tottered into The Firehouse – a little bar and grill that overlooked the beach – at just gone seven, nervous as hell.

What if he didn't show?

What if I made a tit of myself again?

First question answered. He was sat at a table for two away from the bar. Now just to try and keep my shit together.

He had black jeans on with a casual white shirt. I could see a smattering of dark chest hair where the first two buttons were undone.

There was a pint of beer on the table in front of him and the soft glow of the downlight above the table defined his jawline as he looked up.

He looked up and I froze, staring at him. I touched my mouth to check it was closed as he got up and came walking over to me.

'Hey, Saskia,' he said, beaming from ear to ear.

'Hi, Jim,' I said coyly, wondering how I had forgotten just how beautiful he was.

I studied the cocktail list, mostly to compose myself and subdue my nerves so I didn't come out with something stupid this early on.

Unable to make a choice, I settled for a glass of red wine.

I followed him over to the corner of the room.

Guns N' Roses played on the jukebox as I hitched myself up onto the stool.

It was quiet for a Saturday night, but Freddie's would be packed with youngsters, leaving The Firehouse for the older crowd; people who just wanted a quiet pint after a long week at work.

As we sipped our drinks, we chatted. I was surprised at how comfortable and at ease I felt with him.

'So, have you always lived in St Ives?'

'No, I grew up in Cheltenham with my parents and my two older sisters.

My parents are both doctors and met there during their training.'

'What kind of doctors are they?' I asked.

'My mum is a GP and my dad is a paediatrician.'

'Wow, I bet you and your sisters had the best healthcare growing up.'

'You would be surprised!' he chuckled. 'It just meant that I could never fake being ill to get time off school.'

'Have you always lived here?' he asked, taking a sip of his beer.

I watched as the tip of his tongue darted out and over his top lip, licking away the froth, and felt a buzz run through me. How could something so simple have me so on edge with this man?

'Saskia?' he said, gently. Shit, he just asked me a question. Damn it, woman, keep it together.

'No,' I said, sitting back and placing my glass back on the table.

'I grew up just outside Exeter. My dad worked in the bank on the high street most of his life.'

Jim had put his glass down and was giving me his full attention, so I continued.

'My mum worked part time in a supermarket when she wasn't raising my little sister and I.'

'How old is your sister?' he asked.

'Athena is twelve. She was a happy little surprise; she's such a great kid,' I said, smiling.

'So what made you leave Cheltenham?' I asked, hoping I could actually concentrate on what he was saying rather than his mouth this time.

'Well, I realised quite early on that I didn't want to become a doctor; I had a passion for food. I was worried how my parents would take it, but they were really supportive, so I went to college and got my culinary degree.

'After I finished college, I wanted to make sure I was on the right track so I looked around for somewhere I could study Business.'

I sat forward, listening.

'There were so many places to do a business degree, but I wanted somewhere a bit further out, somewhere quiet and peaceful.'

I nodded.

'I always wanted to live by the sea. So I looked at Cornwall College in Camborne and started to look for places to live on the coast. I used to surf with my uncle and we came here a few summers and it was always a favourite of mine.'

'So how long have you lived here?'

'I moved in when I was nineteen, so coming up to seven years now. The deli has been open for five years.'

'We've been neighbours for longer than I realised.

'I actually had some really good news this week,' I told him, desperate to share my excitement with him.

'Oh yeah?' he said, matching my excitement.

'I had a call from Golden Publishing. They want Emily Trevor to do a book signing at my shop!' I practically squealed.

'Wow!' he said. 'She's a pretty big deal. Even I know who she is,' he said, grinning.

'She really is. My sister loves her.'

'My niece Sophie does too. She nagged my sister for days for the new book and has read it twice already.'

'How old is she?' I asked, smiling.

'She's just turned thirteen. She has a little brother, Jake. He's eight, but more into football than reading,' he added affectionately.

'My other sister has a son too. Joe is eighteen now, though, so is generally holed up in his room playing on his computer.' He rolled his eyes.

'Teenage boys eh?' I said, laughing.

'That really is great news, Saskia. What a great way to publicise the shop.'

Eventually we looked up to notice that the bar had started to empty after last orders had been called. Jim drained the dregs from his pint glass and I followed suit.

We walked across the beachfront. It was a little chilly but a beautiful night. The water lapped lazily at the sand as we walked.

'The sky always looks so big from here,' I marvelled, staring up at the tiny dots of light scattered across the clear sky.

'It does,' Jim agreed. 'Nothing in the way to spoil the view,' he said as he slipped his hand in mine.

My skin tingled at his touch, spreading warmth throughout my body and a dopey smile across my face.

We crossed the rest of the beach and walked up the hill until we got to my house.

I was about to invite him in for 'coffee' when he leaned in and gave me a kiss on the cheek.

'Goodnight, Saskia, thank you for a lovely evening.'

I hoped I was hiding my disappointment well enough.

'Goodnight, Jim,' I replied. 'I really enjoyed tonight.'

He waited for me to unlock the front door and step inside, then walked back down the street, turning around and waving.

I stood and watched him until he was out of sight. I could still feel his stubble against my cheek and the woody, masculine smell of his cologne hung in the air around me. It had gone so much better than I had expected, but I was feeling a little deflated at the quick demise of the evening, especially given the walk across the beach had been romantic enough to feature in a novel.

I was feeling happy, but a little disappointed that it had ended there. I was quite partial to a bad boy and it had been such a long time since my last fling.

Still, it had gone well and he certainly seemed second date-worthy. I kept my fingers crossed that he felt the same.

The house was in darkness. Beth was at Ben's, as usual, and Matt was on a stag do for one of the guys he worked with, so would probably stumble back in, drunk, in the early hours.

I stripped off my clothes, laying them over the back of the chair that stood in my room. I pulled on a cotton vest top and pyjama shorts and scraped my hair into a ponytail as I walked across the landing to the bathroom.

Once I had washed away my makeup and cleaned my teeth, I got into bed and picked up my new book, transported to the erotic romance land of my latest read. Within the first few pages, a steamy scene was upon me. As I read about the characters exploring each other with their mouths and hands, my mind conjured thoughts of Jim's hands on me. I read to the end of the scene, feeling heated as their mind-blowing finish was described in great detail.

I marked the page with my tatty old leather bookmark and put it on my bedside table.

Just me and my hands tonight.

I tiptoed my fingers downwards. As my hand brushed my thigh, longing tugged at my core.

I had been so ready to bed that man tonight; the mere thought of him had me on the edge.

I slowly stroked my hand down my slit, shuddering at my own touch, teasing the way I hoped he would.

I closed my eyes, my mind whirling with thoughts about him slowly stripping and fucking me...politely, of course.

Rubbing at my clit, slowly at first, I let out a moan, allowing myself to enjoy the moment. Then, speeding up, I pushed a finger inside, then two, massaging my G-spot.

I cried out as I came hard and fast, dragging out the orgasm for as long as I could.

Rolling over onto my side, I felt spent as I drifted into a deep sleep.

These days I had become an expert at pleasing myself. Someone had to.

Chapter 3

I woke Sunday morning after a great night's sleep. As I yawned and rolled over, I grabbed my phone from the bedside cabinet. The charger wire yanked out as I lay on my back.

I scrolled through the pointless notifications, emails from fast food delivery companies offering discounts and alerts that someone I barely knew from high school had posted another picture on Facebook.

Nothing from Jim.

I don't know what I expected; he was probably still sleeping.

I pictured him asleep and it made me smile.

I waited all day for a text to come through from him, but nothing.

I even stalked him on Instagram to find that, disappointingly, he had been online.

I thought about messaging him, but didn't want to seem too needy so, instead, I took it upon myself to make use of the fast food discount and ordered Chinese for one.

It was mid-morning on Monday by the time the message came through. I almost didn't even look as I was fed up of the disappointment each time my phone beeped but wasn't him.

Hi Saskia. I really enjoyed Saturday night and wondered if you were busy this weekend?

My heart did a little flip when I read it, but then I scolded myself for getting so excited. Casually, or so I hoped, I wrote back.

Hi Jim, I had a nice time too. What were you thinking?

I looked at my phone, waiting to see if he had read the message, but there it sat, unread.

I waited a while, maybe too long, then dragged my eyes from my screen and got on with putting away the delivery of books I had taken in this morning.

As I left the shop to get lunch, I was delighted to see a response from him.

I would like to take you for dinner Saturday.

I thrust my phone inside my pocket and practically skipped to the deli.

Looking handsome as ever, his sleeves were rolled up to his elbows and he was in the middle of serving a couple their food.

I waited in line, watching him, savouring the moment, and then he saw me.

He beamed at me over the counter and I couldn't help but smile back; a stupid, goofy grin.

'I would love to have dinner with you Saturday,' I announced as I got to the front of the queue.

'That's great,' he said as he handed over my food. 'I will message you later to arrange it.'

I paid and left with a huge smile on my face.

Beth had arrived home with fish and chips for us both and

we both sat at the kitchen table eating straight from the paper.

'So tell me about your first date with Salad Guy,' Beth said, stuffing a chip into her mouth.

'It was so nice,' I said, a dreamy look spreading across my face as I recalled the memory.

'Nice?' she scoffed. 'I'm going to need more than that.'

'Well, I don't think I embarrassed myself at all,' I announced proudly, dipping a chip in tomato sauce before biting off a piece and chewing thoughtfully.

'So what is he like?' she probed.

'He's gorgeous and sweet and really—'

'Nice?' Beth finished, laughing.

I slapped her arm playfully, making her drop her chip.

'He's so easy to talk to and we got on really well. He even laughed at my weird jokes.'

Beth grinned, enjoying my happiness.

'His parents are both doctors and he has two sisters,' I babbled as my mind whirred.

'And we walked along the beach. He held my hand.' I blushed a little at how juvenile it sounded, but when I looked up at Beth, she still had a smile plastered across her face.

'Well it all sounds very romance novel,' she said. 'Right up your street.'

'Ah, it really was,' I told her, unable to get the goofy grin off my face.

'So...' She paused for effect. 'What happened after the romantic beach stroll?'

My smile faltered. 'He walked me to the front door, kissed me on the cheek and left.'

'A true gent,' she said, giggling at my disappointment.

I stuck out my bottom lip. 'Yeah. I was kind of hoping he wouldn't be though.'

'Well maybe he wants to build it up a bit first. Take it slowly. Isn't that what your book boyfriends do?'

'Yeah, I suppose so,' I said, scrunching up the chip paper and tossing it in the bin.

'So have you set the next date?'

'Yes,' I told her, my smile returning. 'We are going out again tomorrow.'

'See, I told you that you needed to speak to guys in order to find one,' she said proudly.

Beth jumped up and turned up the radio. 'I love this song!' she said, dancing around the kitchen.

'You want to go out dancing?' she asked.

'What, now?' I shot back, horrified.

'Yes!' she laughed. 'Remember when we used to be spontaneous and go out any night of the week?'

'Yeah...but...'

'It's Friday night, Sass!' She cut me off, laughing. 'Come on, I want to dance.'

'But I have a date tomorrow!' I protested.

'What, you need to be in bed by nine because you have a date? You are such a nanna!' she laughed, giving me a light punch in the arm.

I sat and thought about it for a short time before agreeing.

'Come on then, I want to dance too. Not too late though, I have work before my date.'

We did a quick half an hour hair and makeup dash, changed into skirts and tops, then pulled on heels and jackets before heading out of the door.

'The spontaneous nights always were the best ones.' I grinned as we sashayed up the street towards Bar Bella.

We squeezed through masses of people and headed towards the bar. It was busier than Freddie's on a Friday night. Clearly Bar Bella was the place to be.

The queue at the bar was at least three people deep, but was moving quickly. We got a bottle of wine and two glasses and I followed Beth to a table she had spotted near the dancefloor.

We took our seats and I opened the Pinot, pouring the chilled liquid into both of our glasses.

Beth and I had been to Bar Bella once before a few years back and it hadn't changed much.

It was very modern, mostly black and white but with bright colours thrown in around the place. The toilets were what I remembered most. There were mirrors everywhere
you looked and navigating them after one too many drinks turned into something from a fun house, although not so fun.

The music was loud and the atmosphere was heading towards a nightclub feel rather than a wine bar vibe.

There was a group of younger girls dancing next to their table, singing along to the 90s mix that was pouring from the speakers. They were dressed in tiny skirts and cropped tops, and were having the time of their lives.

A few young guys watched them, practically drooling. I couldn't hear what they were saying, but they appeared to be encouraging one lad in the group to go and dance with the girls.

I turned my attention back to Beth, the frustration from my evening with Jim clouding my mind again.

I was so sure I was getting him in the house,' I told Beth. 'I had him at my front door and was about to invite him in when he moved in for a kiss.'

Beth sat waiting for me to continue.

'Then he went and kissed me on the cheek. And he smelled *so* good,' I finished, eyes squeezed shut, remembering the woody, masculine scent as he had leaned in to kiss me.

'Well,' she ventured, 'maybe he is just a gentleman. You know, a good guy. Maybe he doesn't fuck on the first date.'

'Yeah I know, and that's good.' I tried to convince myself. 'But he is so damn hot.'

Beth laughed. 'Well what about tomorrow? Where is he taking you?'

'We're going to that little restaurant in town, you know, the little boutique one? It's called Cellar Bistro, I think.'

Beth nodded and mmmd as she drank her wine.

'Ben took me there a couple of months ago, it was divine.'

'Well I'm hopeful that I will get at least a decent kiss from him, even if he is a complete gent., otherwise—'

Beth cut me off, shushing me. 'You will never guess who just walked in,' she said, wide- eyed.

As I turned around, Jim had already seen me and was making his way over. He looked effortlessly gorgeous, as always, in a casual blue shirt and jeans.

'Hello, ladies. Fancy seeing you here, Saskia,' he said with genuine surprise.

I couldn't help my smile as he kissed me on the cheek.

'Hi, Jim, what a lovely surprise,' I said, beaming. 'This is my housemate, Beth,' I said, gesturing to Beth, who was grinning at the situation.

'Well, I have known her since we were four, but housemate will do.' She laughed. 'Nice to meet you, Jim.'

Jim shook her hand and turned to his friend.

'This is Scott, a friend of mine, we used to work together.'

Scott waved and grinned at Beth. She was used to most men drooling over her and I'm not even sure she noticed half the time.

'We will leave you ladies to your evening,' Jim said. 'I will see you tomorrow, Saskia.' He leaned in and kissed me on the cheek, his intoxicating cedar scent lightly mixed with alcohol. As he pulled away, his eyes were dark and promising.

'Yes, you will,' I replied with a smile. 'Nice to meet you, Scott.'

They left and I exhaled as they did.

'Wow, Sass,' Beth said. 'He is hotter than I remember, and he is so into you.'

'Do you really think so?' I demanded as I watched them sitting at a table in the corner, only just in view.

'The sexual tension in here!' she said, fanning her face.

I tried my hardest not to look over at Jim, in case he saw me staring, but he seemed to get more gorgeous every time I saw him.

It was so hard to concentrate with him sat over there; I could feel his eyes searing into me as I tried to stay focused on what Beth was saying.

As the bar got busier, I lost sight of them in the crowd and managed to relax into our evening a little more.

Once we had finished our bottle, Beth picked up the cocktail menu and started reeling off our order to the barman.

I excused myself and went to the toilet, fixing my hair and

re-applying my red lip gloss in the crazy mirrored room afterwards.

I managed to pick the right door to get out, but was still feeling a little disorientated as I left the toilet.

The men's toilet door opened as I walked past it and there stood Jim.

'Hello again,' I said, tucking my hair behind my ear, then pulling it back out again awkwardly.

'Hi, Saskia.' He looked a little more relaxed and possibly a little drunk.

'I didn't tell you how beautiful you look this evening.'

I blushed as he tucked the stray hair back behind my ear.

'Thank you, you look very lovely too,' I managed.

'I'm really looking forward to tomorrow night, Saskia.'

'Me too. I've not been there before, but Beth says the restaurant is really nice and we had a great time the other night and...' I was doing it again, but he didn't seem to

notice. He just stood there, staring at me with that new dark look in his eyes.

'Not sure I want to wait that long,' he said, catching me off guard.

I gave a nervous giggle and looked down at my feet as I felt my face flush.

Suddenly his thumb was at my chin, moving my face up to look at him. He was very close now and I could see the five o'clock shadow appearing on his beautiful face.

He moved in, still cupping my chin and the smell of his aftershave made me dizzy.

He kissed me, so slowly and lightly I felt my knees go weak underneath me.

Just as I started to kiss him back, his lips left mine and he ran his hand down my face.

'I have wanted to do that for the longest time, Saskia,' he whispered as he stepped away from me.

I had no words; I just stood there.

'Come on, they will be wondering where we have gone,' he said, straightening his shirt.

I nodded and followed him as he walked back towards the bar.

'Where have you been?' Beth asked, slurring her words a little as I sat back at the bar. 'I got you your favourite, Piña Colada.'

'He kissed me,' was all I could muster.

'What, just now?' she demanded, looking more serious.

'Yes, he was coming out of the toilet and he kissed me.' I grinned at the memory.

'And?'

'And I really can't wait for tomorrow night!' I laughed, starting to regain my composure.

'So, I guess we're staying here?' I gestured to the cocktails lined up.

'Oh yeah. I thought: we're having fun, why bother going anywhere else, right? I got us shots, too.' She pushed a Jägerbomb in my direction and picked up hers.

They went down in quick succession and we moved onto our cocktails.

We had nearly made our way through them when Beth disappeared to the toilets.

A few minutes later, she came back looking a little worse for wear.

'I need to go home, Sass,' she said.

‘I’m going to phone Ben and see if he will come get us.’

‘Oh dear!’ I laughed. She loved a drink, but never learned. ‘Of course, go give him a ring.’

I chuckled to myself as Beth walked back towards the toilet for some quiet to call Ben.

Feeling brave, I got my phone out and typed a message to Jim.

I’m looking forward to tomorrow evening, especially after that little teaser.

I looked down at my phone as it vibrated. I stole a look over at Jim and his friend; I could see them now the crowds had dispersed, but he wasn’t looking back.

I stared at the message and read it a few times, just to make sure I had it right.

So are you always this polite or would you let me tie you up and fuck you till you’re sore?

I looked over again. This time he was looking right at me.

Excitement buzzed around me at lightning speed as we made eye contact.

He was zipping up his hooded jacket and getting up to leave.

I was already on my feet when Beth got back to the table.

‘Is Ben coming to get you?’

‘Yeah, he will be here in a few minutes. I’ll get him to drop you off, then go back with him, if that’s OK?’

I grinned. ‘No need, I think I have a place to stay.’

Beth followed my gaze to Jim, waiting at the door.

‘Finally!’ she said, and slapped my arse as we walked towards Jim.

Ben was outside by the time I had managed to get Beth’s coat on her and to the door.

The chill of the night air made me shiver as I opened the car door and manoeuvred her into the passenger seat.

'Have fun,' she slurred as she fell into the passenger seat of Ben's Mercedes-Benz.

'You too. Look after her, Ben,' I said, shaking my head.

'I will,' Ben said, looking mock-disapprovingly at his mess of a girlfriend. 'Sure you don't need a lift?'

'I'm fine, thanks.' I closed the door, tapping it to signal them to go.

I felt Jim step closer in behind me as he slid his arms around my waist, pulling me back against him. His warmth instantly stilled my shivering as he rested his chin on the top of my head.

We watched Beth and Ben drive away before I turned to face him. I tipped my head back and looked at his perfect face; our mouths just inches apart. I was so ready to taste his lips again, but as I got lost in those dark eyes, he came to stand next to me, putting his arm around my lower back and his hand lightly at my hip.

Inside, I was jumping up and down with excitement. On the outside I was doing a very good job of looking calm and walking in heels.

As we walked, so many delicious smells poured from the doorways of the fast food restaurants, people spilling out into the street to sate alcohol-fuelled hunger.

Light from the shop fronts illuminated the streets and its occupants. The noise level wasn't far off that of the clubs and bars, with people shouting to each other; drink having remove any filter they may previously have had.

Jim looked over at me and I noticed the sparkle in his eyes.

I felt alive with nervous excitement as we walked through

the harbour.

We stopped outside a little gift store opposite the harbour wall and Jim unlocked a door to the left of the shop front.

We climbed two sets of stairs and he unlocked another door to his apartment. He closed the door and turned to me. 'Fuck, you're beautiful,' he said, through almost gritted teeth.

Excitement rippled through me.

Gently cupping my face, he lifted my lips close to his, kissing me so gently I thought I would melt.

Pushing me backwards slowly, he held his hand on my chest until I hit the lounge wall with a light thud.

His kiss deepened, his tongue more urgently searching my mouth.

I heard ragged breathing and realised it was my own.

His lips grazed my neck as he kissed and nibbled my skin. He planted his hands on the wall either side of my shoulders and pressed himself against me.

He undid his fly and rolled on a condom, then lifted my dress and pulled my underwear to the side.

I stole a quick glance at his sheathed dick, long and thick, before he pushed up inside me, the searing pain quickly turning to pleasure.

It was happening so fast, and rough.

I realised how wet I was for him.

He fucked me hard against the lounge wall, bringing me so close to climax, but emptying himself moments before I could finish.

He pulled out and steadied me with one hand. Without even making eye contact, he turned away and walked off to dispose of the condom.

I put my knickers back in place and pulled my skirt back down.

I was still damn horny and annoyed that I didn't get mine.

My brain was yelling: what the fuck?

He appeared back at my side and took my hand, leading me to the kitchen where he poured me a glass of white wine. I took a sip and the crisp ,cold liquid revitalised me.

The kitchen was very different to my own; expensive-looking, sparkly worktops, slate flooring and cupboards that shone under the LED lights with their glossy finish.

Still saying nothing, he took my arm and I followed him through his bedroom to a beautiful en suite.

There was a huge tub and a shower big enough for an orgy. He stood behind me, kissing my shoulders. Instantly, I heated and felt a tingle rush between my legs. He slowly pulled my dress off my shoulders and slid it down until it was on the floor and I was in my underwear. Thankfully a new set I had bought earlier that week; a pale-pink lace bra with matching thong. He started the shower and removed his t-shirt and jeans.

Seeing him for the first time in nothing but his boxers was breath-taking.

His broad shoulders and strong arms gave way to his slight waist. He wasn't bulky and muscly, but had beautifully chiselled abs and pecs, covered with a light smattering of dark hairs. His black boxers were resting low on his hips and just above the waistband was a perfect V.

I let my eyes roam over him, each bit of him better than the last. He stood for a while as if to let me get my fill, undressing me with his eyes.

His package bulged; I was desperate to look and touch and taste.

He turned on the shower and stepped inside, taking me with him.

I was about to ask why we still had our underwear on, but he cut me off by kissing me. He ran his hands over my breasts through my soaking wet bra.

He undid the clasp, letting them fall, licking his way to my nipples, sucking them and sending shockwaves downwards.

He took a step back and looked down. He traced the outline of my slit through my sodden and now completely transparent panties.

Seconds later, he was on his knees, water cascading over his head as he sucked at my clit through the wet lace, taking me right back to the almost-climactic state he had left me in.

With his hands on my breasts, he licked his way along the edge of my panties, finding a way in and straight up inside me.

The sudden, expert intrusion had me cumming into his mouth almost instantly; I shuddered violently.

He stood up and kissed me, his tongue searching my mouth, pushing his hands back into my knickers.

'I'm done, give me a minute!' I protested, my legs shaking as I grabbed onto his arms for support.

'No, I'll decide when you're done.'

He was right; still feeling the aftershocks from my last orgasm, the next one came rolling in, even more intense than the first.

I bit my bottom lip as I cried out, the intensity taking me by surprise.

He lifted me up and carried me out of the shower, wrapped

me in a fluffy bath robe and placed me on the bed.

He looked like he had just stepped off the cover of *Men's Health*.

Droplets from his wet tousled hair ran down his perfectly tanned and toned body.

His towel was wrapped around his waist and that sexy V of sculpted abs peeked out above it.

I followed the drops of water with my finger and came to rest at the top of his towel.

I gave a little tug and the towel fell to the floor, revealing an uncircumcised porn-worthy cock, hard and ready for the next round.

I licked my lips greedily and pulled him towards me.

Sitting on the end of his bed, while he stood, my head level with his glorious cock, I went to work.

Teasing him first with my fingers, then my tongue, licking light trails up and down his length, I purposely avoided the tip until he grabbed my head with both hands and sunk himself deep into my mouth, groaning with pleasure as he did.

Over and over I took his shaft as deep and quick as I could without gagging until I felt his muscles stiffen and his breath quicken.

I sped up and he pumped my mouth full of his warm, salty cum. I swallowed it down and we both lay side by side on the bed.

I woke to the sound of the bedroom door opening, my throat dry. I was still naked, but covered with a throw.

Jim was wearing a pair of light Levi's and carrying a tray. My stomach was doing somersaults at the smell of the food; my mind was fighting over whether to devour him or the food first.

Hangover starting to kick in, my stomach won and we sat in bed eating cheese and bacon toasties and drinking tea.

How could I feel so comfortable with him already?

When we'd finished eating, he lifted the throw and looked my naked body up and down. My breath caught in my throat.

'You like being looked at?' he asked, catching me off guard.

'Um, I've never really thought about it.'

'I think you do,' he said, sparkle back in his eyes. He climbed on top of me and, to my surprise, pushed easily inside me.

Had his mere gaze been enough to light my fires and melt me so that I was ready to take him again?

We fucked lazily, his arms taking his weight with every thrust. Our skin fused together, laced with sweat and the smell of aftershave on his skin set my senses alight. He pushed deeper, hitting that sweet spot until I was helpless to do anything other than let him bring me to a shuddering finish, perfectly timed with his.

He rolled over, removed the condom, knotted it and dropped it into the bin next to the bed, then pulled me in to spoon against his chest, his still half-erect dick fitting neatly into my arse-crack.

'I'm not sure I can move!' I laughed, unable to even open my eyes.

'Do you need to move?' he asked.

'Should I not go home?' I said tentatively.

'Do you want to go home?'

'Not really,' I answered.

'Then you don't need to move,' he said, pulling me closer into him.

The feelings of anger and confusion that had followed our first encounter that evening were well and truly gone, leaving me warm and sated. He kissed my head and there we stayed till morning.

Chapter 4

'Good morning.' Jim smiled down at me as I opened my eyes the next morning.

He sat on the bed next to me and put two plates of pastries down.

He was already dressed and ready for work.

As I sat up, I noticed a mug of coffee on the table next to the bed.

'Morning.' I smiled back at him, trying to stifle a yawn.

'You looked peaceful, but I didn't want you to be late for work.'

'Thank you,' I said, looking at my phone to see that it was only 6.30 a.m.

I expected awkwardness, but there was none.

'I hope I didn't drag you away last night,' Jim said, looking a little guilty.

I laughed. 'No, Beth was definitely ready to leave.'

'That's OK then. It took all my willpower to wait as long as I did. When I walked into Bella and saw you, I couldn't keep away. I really tried to leave you to your night, but you looked good enough to eat in that little skirt.'

I looked across to find him staring into my soul again with those dark, brooding eyes.

‘Well, I’m glad you didn’t wait any longer,’ I muttered, feeling a blush creep up my face.

We finished our breakfast and I got dressed in last night’s clothes.

‘I’ll drop you back before I open up if you like?’ Jim said.

Stepping back into my heels, the soles of my feet screamed in agony.

‘That would be lovely, I’m not sure my feet will carry me this morning.’ I laughed.

Jim pulled up outside my house and leaned over to me, his face close to mine.

‘I’ll see you this evening for dinner.’ His breath was minty-fresh on my face.

I was thankful I’d used some of his mouthwash as his lips then brushed against mine. The kiss was gentle at first, then became a little more urgent before he broke away.

I opened my eyes.

‘I’m looking forward to it,’ I said with a grin.

‘I’ll pick you up at seven!’ he called out of the open window before he drove away.

I opened my front door to the smell of bacon and remembered that Matt had a day off today.

I found him in the kitchen, dressed in joggers and a t shirt.

Matt had moved into our neighbourhood when Beth and I were around eight years old. His family had bought the house next door to Beth and he very quickly became our favourite person. Unlike the other boys in our school, he wasn’t disgusted by girls and was always happy to join in our gossip sessions.

As we all got older, rumours flew around about the three of us being so close.

A guy and two girls could never just be friends, surely!

But that's what we were. He became like a protective older brother to us both and our friendship continued through our teens when we all left home and decided we should live together.

He was stocky and tall with hair so dark it looked black, and bright-blue eyes.

Charm seemed to radiate from him; his easy-go-lucky nature was infectious, and, at over six foot tall, he towered over a shorty like me. He folded me up into one of his bear hugs, 'Hey, Sass, I feel like I haven't seen you properly in ages,' he said as he put me back down on the kitchen floor.

'It's only been a few days,' I informed him, 'but that's what happens when you only pop home to pick up clean clothes...' I chastised him sweetly.

'Ah, Sass, I've got loads to tell you, I—'

'You had sex!' he almost shouted. 'It's written all over your face.'

I laughed at him. I could never get anything past him.

'I'll tell you all about it tomorrow evening, promise. I'll make dinner, but, right now, I need to go open the shop and I have another hot date tonight.' I winked.

Jenny was extra cheery today. She had just finished a book I had recommended and was dying to talk about it.

'Oh I loved Sylvie's character so much,' she mused. 'I was so team Brad all the way.'

'Ah, I know. He was so much better than Dan.' I laughed.

'Oh and the ending.' She looked at me with big eyes.

I laughed. 'Tell me about it. I have read that she is writing the second in the series.'

'Thank God for that!' she said, visibly relieved. 'It couldn't end like that.'

I loved her sweet-natured personality and really enjoyed her company on Saturdays. She reminded me a little of what Athena may be like as a young adult.

It was already gone six and Jim was picking me up at seven. But I was still standing in my towel in front of my wardrobe deciding what to wear.

It had been an unusually warm spring day, so I took a light-blue cami dress out of my wardrobe.

I removed the towel to get dressed, but caught sight of myself in the full-length mirror. I stared for a while, taking in each part, trying to see it how he does. I spread my legs a little and realised that even looking at myself got me going. Jeez, what had he unleashed?

I finally pushed the thoughts aside and got dressed, sweeping my hair over my shoulder and braiding it down to breast height, noting that it was definitely time for a trim.

I heard the car pull up outside and was at the front door before he had even turned the engine off.

'Hi, you,' Jim greeted me as I got in the car.

'Hey, yourself,' I said, pulling my seatbelt across my chest and clipping it in.

'You look beautiful, as always,' he told me with a smile.

I thanked him, blushing a little at his compliment.

We chatted easily on the short drive to the restaurant and were directed to the bar for a drink while the table was prepared.

Cellar Bistro was a quaint little restaurant with a contemporary feel.

Everything about the place was mismatched to perfection, from the table mats down to the chairs around the tables. There were odd little ornaments and pictures around the walls.

If I had attempted this, it would look a right mess, but whoever had completed the decor here was a genius!

We ordered meals with posh names that arrived as tiny portions on little plates. I wondered if we would leave hungry, but, by the end of three courses, I felt comfortably full.

'So how tired were you today, then?' he asked, smiling.

'Uh, well, I only fell asleep once before lunch,' I joked.

'Yeah, I was pretty tired too.' He laughed. 'It was worth it though.' His eyes sparkled with mischief and I blushed, remembering our late-night antics.

We laughed and chatted until Jim asked for the bill.

We walked to the car park and I climbed into his 4x4 beside him.

'I'm not ready to go home.'

'Oh, I know you're not,' he said with a smile. He started up the car and drove out of the car park and along the main road.

Placing his hand on my thigh, he gently started to stroke my leg up and down over my skirt.

I looked over at him, but his eyes were still looking ahead. His hands crept slowly under my skirt, circling the edge of my thong, grazing my already damp mound.

'Take them off,' he spoke without even looking at me.

I did as I was told and removed my knickers, letting them fall to the floor. My heartbeat sped up in anticipation as he started to undo his trousers.

Naked under my skirt and desperate for his touch,

I watched as he pulls out his cock, already hard.

I don't need an invitation;

I want him in my mouth.

I lean over and slowly trace my tongue around the tip, feeling him stiffen at my touch.

I remind him to keep his eyes on the road then deepthroat him, my head buried in his lap. I take him in my mouth over and over again until my eyes are watering.

He pulls over into a layby and grabs my hair, pushing my head down on his cock; fucking my mouth. His low, guttural noises spur me on.

He lifts my head up and kisses me before pulling me sideways on, one leg over the driver seat and into the back of the car.

He holds me in place with my legs spread, and I'm breathless. He's looking at me again and he was right; I fucking love it.

He starts to lick up my thighs, then teases his tongue across my clit.

Dizzy from excitement, the world around me seems to melt away.

I felt my orgasm start to build as he thrusts his tongue inside me. Dripping wet and coming in his mouth, I barely register that we may be seen.

He opens his door and gets out of the car, so I climb across the seats to follow him like a dog following its master.

It's getting dark and he bends me over the bonnet and lifts my skirt, revealing my bare arse.

I feel embarrassed, like a naughty schoolgirl about to be

spanked, and the effect it has on me is exquisite.

Holding me down with one hand, he slaps my arse with the other as I start to squirm, gushing a little down my thighs.

Pushing my legs apart, he eases his fingers inside me.

He stops and holds me face down for what feels like an eternity.

Then I feel the tip of his cock teasing my pussy. I try to push back onto him but I am being made to wait.

'I need more,' I begged him. He groaned and I felt his cock strain at my opening. So he likes it when I beg, I think to myself, making a mental note, desperate to please this man however I can.

'I know you do.' He grunted. 'But you will wait.' His voice is gruff and dominating.

Finally he fills me, making the wait so worthwhile.

Fucking me hard from behind, his hand finds my clit.

I'm moaning and coming hard. I try and move his hand but I should know by now that he decides when I'm done.

Within seconds I'm coming again, even more intensely this time, perfectly teamed with his orgasm

Sitting on the bonnet of his car, my head on his chest, he looks down at me.

'This is good, right? I don't just mean the sex.'

I smile up at him and agree.

'Yes, this is good, very good.'

Beth is waiting up when I arrive home, having emptied a bottle of wine or two, desperate for details as I had given very little away in my texts.

'I need to put my PJs on,' I tell her. 'Then you will have a blow-by-blow account. Pun very much intended.'

We stayed up talking till the sun came up with tea and biscuits to keep us going.

She squealed with delight when I told her how we had gone from friend zone to fuck frenzy in 0.6 seconds.

'Honestly, it was so worth the wait.'

'Well I'm glad to hear you finally got in his pants, and that gentleman Jim is no longer a gent.'

Chapter 5

The sun streaming through my window woke me just after nine the following morning. Not even my dark-grey curtains could keep it out. Shadows played across the maple desk where my laptop sat open. My clothes from the night before were hanging over the chair pushed under the desk.

After just a handful of hours' sleep, I was surprisingly full of energy and ready to start my day.

I pulled on my gym kit and headed into the kitchen to fill my water bottle.

Beth was sat at the kitchen table staring into an empty coffee cup. 'Gym?' I asked, not convinced I had won her over.

'Urgh, bed more like it,' she said, putting her head on her hands.

'Tea tonight then? Matt's here too. Wants to know all about my new man.' I smiled.

Beth gave me two thumbs up without lifting her head off the table.

After an hour and a half in the gym – feeling quite proud that I had made it through a spin class and was still managing to walk – I wandered around the supermarket, humming along to the music that crept out from the shop speaker system while I filled the trolley with everything I needed for tonight's tea. It had been a long time since the three of us had sat down together properly and I was feeling happier than I had been in for a long time.

I hadn't stopped smiling for days.

I pottered round the kitchen, preparing the vegetables as the chicken roasted in the oven and singing along to The Corrs on the radio. Dinner was almost ready when Matt arrived home.

I could hear the shower running so knew Beth was over the worst of her hangover.

The three of us ate and talked about Beth and Ben, me and Jim, and how things were really hotting up with Matt and his girlfriend Stacey.

They had been dating for around four months now and we still hadn't met her.

'We should have dinner.' I grinned. 'The six of us. We can do a course each. I'll take dessert!' Beth and Matt agreed and we set a date to check with our retrospective partners.

Jim and I had only been on a handful of dates, was it too soon?

No sooner had I suggested it, then I started to regret the idea.

After clearing away the dishes, we had sat on the sofa, arguing what to watch on TV.

'Come on, girls,' Matt groaned as we won the battle for the remote and put re-runs of *Gossip Girl* on. 'Ah, you know you love it, Matt.' Beth goaded.

'That's one secret I'll never tell.' After just one episode, the lack of sleep started to catch up on me so I excused myself and went up to bed.

I looked at my phone just as it started to ring. It was Jim. My heart did a little flip as I left it a ring or two before answering.

'Hey, Sass. I hope it's not a bad time to call you, I was just thinking about you...' Jim's sexy voice poured through the phone.

'Hey, you. Of course not. It's lovely to hear from you.' I was glad he couldn't see the stupid grin plastered across my face.

I lay on my bed with my feet up against the wall like I did as a teenager. 'How was your day?'

'It was good, thank you. I've not really done much, I was definitely ready for a day off work. How was yours?'

'Quite quiet, too. I managed to get to the gym though.

I'm really hoping that the book signing with Emily Trevor next week will get some publicity for the book shop.'

'I'm sure it will," he said. 'An event like that will bring loads of people in.'

'And all the holidaymakers will be down soon enough.'

I mmed in agreement, trying to be brave enough to tell him about the dinner plans.

'I was wondering if you would like to come here for dinner next week? Beth is bringing Ben and Matt is going to finally introduce us to Stacey.'

'That sounds great, Saskia, I would love to.'

We said goodnight and I ended the call feeling like nothing could bring me down from this high.

It was Monday again, and I had been so busy getting the shop ready for the signing tomorrow that I had skipped lunch altogether.

I tidied all of the shelves, rearranging the genres to

showcase the children's books around the front. I put out a chair and table for Emily and made sure there was plenty of space for the show boards the company had told me they would be bringing.

I scrubbed and dusted, making sure everything was spotless and perfect.

It was just after four when the little bell rang above the door to announce a customer.

I looked up to see Jim walking over to me with a bag in his hand. 'I figured you were too busy for lunch. I had to wait till the lunchtime rush was over, but I closed up a little early and brought you something to eat.' He was grinning from ear to ear.

'Thank you so much!' I said, his grin infectious. 'I'm starving.'

'It's my pleasure,' he said. 'I can bring some nibbles to the shop tomorrow for the signing if you like?'

'Oh, really?' I asked, taken back by his kindness.

'Of course,' he said, smiling and showing his beautifully straight, white teeth.

He stayed with me until closing time, helping me make sure everything was ready for the morning.

'Can I take you home and make you dinner?' 'How can I refuse that?'

His apartment was as lovely as I remembered. Really modern and bigger than my house.

It was very tastefully decorated and minimalistic without feeling cold and bare.

I wandered around the kitchen, admiring his extensive collection of cookery books.

'Would you like a drink?'

'Tea please.'

Jim led me through to the front room carrying both mugs and handed me mine as I gazed out of the huge window that overlooked the harbour.

'Wow, what a view,' I said, genuinely taken by the beautiful sight.

'It's the reason I bought the apartment,' he said, standing behind me.

He was so close I could feel the heat from his body. His cedar scent was filling my senses, making me heady.

'Looking forward to tomorrow?' he asked, leading me to sit next to him on the sofa.

The plush cushions folded me in closer to him.

'Yes, I really am,' I said, scolding myself for the fact that tomorrow was far from my mind. How could I think of anything else while he sat beside me, so close his thigh was touching mine.

I shifted a little and rested my hand on my leg, brushing his lightly.

'Jim?' I said, my voice sounding like it didn't even belong to me. 'There's something I have been wondering about.'

He looked a little concerned. 'Please, go on,' he said politely.

'Well...' I started, not sure I wanted to finish. 'You remember that text you sent me that night at Freddie's?' He nodded, and licked his top lip. 'Well, you said something, and...' Embarrassment stopped me from completing my sentence.

He smiled, eyes sparkling.

'You want me to tie you up?'

I looked down at the table, feeling the blush creep up on me, unable to look him in the eye.

Without another word, he took my hand and led me into his bedroom.

The huge bed took the focus in the centre of the biggest wall of the bedroom, neatly made with crisp white sheets.

'I didn't want to scare you off,' he explained as he tucked his hand underneath the mattress and pulled out leather straps at all four corners.

I wasn't shocked and certainly wasn't scared. In fact, I was quite the opposite.

'Have you been tied up before?'

'A few times,' I admitted, 'but a long time ago.' Memories came to mind of my college boyfriend tying me up and blindfolding me, only to lose his erection halfway through, then blaming me, saying I made everything awkward. I pushed them back down and locked them away like always. I didn't want them to ruin this moment.

'And you want me to do this?' He was looking very serious as I nodded.

'Give me a safe word.'

'A safe word?'

'Yes, if at any point you don't feel comfortable, just tell me and I will stop. OK?'

My mind froze, what could I use as a safe word?

He was looking at me for an answer and I had forgotten all words.

Shakespeare, my mouth told him without my brain's assistance.

He smiled in acknowledgment. 'Shakespeare it is.'

He stripped me as I stood there, slowly kissing me, then laid me on my back in the middle of the bed.

He walked around me, pulling one hand at a time over my head and cuffing my wrists to the bed.

Moving round to my feet, he spread my legs one at a time, opening me up to him and placing the cuffs around my ankles.

He stood there staring. 'You are so damn beautiful, Saskia. You enjoying me looking at you, but not as much as I enjoy the view.'

His words and my helplessness had me hotter than ever. He teased and kissed me, running his lips up my thighs. Then he put his mouth on me and I came almost instantly. Pleased with his work, he released the restraints and turned me over onto my front, re-tying my hands. With my face in the pillow, he pushed my knees into my chest and pulled my ass up so I was on full display for him. He admired the view for a while, his breathing quickening. Practically dripping at the thought of him staring at my pussy, I was ready for him.

He put his mouth back on me again, trailing his tongue over my clit.

Paying attention to my moans, he started to speed up, licking and sucking, then moved his tongue upwards, slowly flicking his tongue over my arsehole.

I pulled at my wrist restraints, not sure how to feel about this. I'd had anal sex with my last boyfriend and never really enjoyed it much, but no one had ever done this.

He was testing me now, giving my arse the full attention of his tongue.

Moving past the weirdness, it felt good...really good.

I found myself thrusting back onto his mouth. Suddenly his hand was back at my clit, rubbing furiously as his tongue did a number on my arse and bringing me to a quick finish again.

He freed my wrists as I lay there panting, my orgasm still rippling through me.

My mind full of him, I started to pull at his clothes.

I pushed him onto the bed and lightly ran my fingers across his jawline and down to his chest. His cock hardened, rising up in a plea to be touched.

I continued my fingers travelling down that little line of pubic hair and stroke his full length, right up to the tip.

I follow this pattern again but with my tongue, delicately grazing the head.

I take all of him into my mouth and feel him inhale sharply; looking up at him so I can watch how much he needs my mouth.

He pulls out, getting to his feet and sits me on the end of the bed, standing in front of me.

Gently he eases himself back in, slowly filling my mouth, getting in every inch he can.

Taking control, he holds my wrists together in my lap and fucks my mouth until he's at the brink of orgasm.

He flips me back onto my knees and, instinctively, I display myself for him again.

He reaches through my legs and strokes his hand back across my sex as I moan and beg him for more.

He pulls on a condom and rubs his dick against my clit, pulling away as I try desperately to sit back onto him.

'Please, James,' I beg.

'What do you want, Saskia?' he asks, hoarsely.

'I need you inside me,' I choke out.

He waits a moment, enjoying my desperation, then guides himself inside me, filling me up.

Too good to go slow, he fucks me hard, hitting that sweet spot every time.

As I hit an earth-shattering climax, I clamp down all around him, panting and pushing back against him. He moans loudly and grips my hips as I felt him coming inside me.

We lay next to each other on the bed for a while, unable to move. My mind is blown.

With all the strength I have left, I lift my head to look at him.

'I'm sure you said you were making me dinner.'

He slaps my bare arse and rolls off the side of the bed, wandering into the en suite.

He emerged a few minutes later. 'See you down there, miss, don't be long.' And with that, he was gone.

I dragged myself into the en suite for a freshen up and got dressed as quickly as I could.

As I opened the bedroom door, the smell hit me and I remembered; this man has culinary expertise. I was in for a treat.

He did not disappoint.

After a beautiful dinner of lamb lollipops with little diced potatoes and the nicest, most tender vegetables I had ever tasted, I was seriously wondering how we were supposed to cook for him.

We were cosied up on his sofa after dinner, listening to music when he asked, 'So, how was your evening, Saskia?'

I lifted my head off his chest to look at him 'Best yet.'

Jim had dropped me home relatively early so I could get a full night sleep before the big day tomorrow.

I fell into bed and drifted off into the best sleep I’d had in ages.

Chapter 6

I'd set my alarm an hour earlier so I had plenty of time to potter about in the shop and make sure everything was perfect.

Beth had taken the day off to help out and was walking sleepily towards the bathroom as I emerged fresh as a daisy after my shower. She mumbled a greeting on her way and pulled on the light cord, grumbling and hiding her eyes from the harsh light.

'Thank you so much for being here today. If it's as busy as I hope it will be, I'm definitely going to need the extra pair of hands' I said. 'Are you sure you don't have better things to do with your holiday days?'

'Not at all,' she said, shaking her head. 'I have so many banked with all the overtime I've been doing, and I'm so proud of you. My Sass, having a famous author at her store. I wouldn't miss this for the world.

'And you're buying me breakfast, right?' she added, lightly punching my arm.

An hour later, we were both in the car, having decided to pick up breakfast on the way in.

It didn't take the two of us long to go back over everything, ensuring the shop was ready for my special guest and we were on our second coffee by the time she arrived.

Emily Trevor was a YA author who had written a few books but become increasingly popular since her latest book, *Nun Tales*.

It was about a children's home run by nuns and, even as an adult, I had thoroughly enjoyed it.

She breezed into the shop like a gust of fresh air. She was taller than I had imagined and not a hair was out of place on her blonde bobbed crop.

She was dressed in a casual trouser suit and looked positively glowing. She shook my hand warmly.

'Hi, Saskia, it's so lovely to meet you. Thank you for having me here today.'

I was quite starstruck. Emily Trevor was here, in *my* little bookshop.

'Emily, you are so welcome, I think it's me who should be thanking you.' The words tumbled out as I continued to shake her hand.

She smiled and I released her hand.

'Your shop is beautiful,' she said, looking around. 'I love the reading areas.'

I followed, hanging on her every word.

'Thank you so much.' I beamed.

Beth appeared from the back of the shop and confidently strode up to us.

'Hi, I'm Beth. I'm a friend of Saskia's. Lovely to meet you.'

Beth shook Emily's hand.

'Can I get you something to drink Emily?'

'Tea would be lovely, milk and one sugar please.'

I watched as she continued to browse the shelves.

It was like Mary Poppins herself had just called by the shop.

Instantly, I really liked her; it was impossible not to.

The morning flew by with so many people coming in for signed copies. My little shop had never been so full.

Jim had dropped off trays of mini wraps and platters of fresh fruit which were going down a storm and Emily was wowing everyone.

The laughter and excitement of children and teenagers filled the room. I marvelled at how patiently they waited their turn to see their idol and how their faces lit up as she greeted them.

Even the parents were taken by her.

I stood back and tried to commit everything about the moment to memory.

When 3pm rolled around, Emily thanked me and seemed genuinely grateful, though I think I owed her more thanks for putting Just One More Chapter on the map.

Once she had left, Beth and I started to clear up, the shop suddenly feeling very empty and quiet.

As I settled down into bed, flicking through new series on Netflix, my phone rang next to me. I smiled when I saw Jim's name appear on my screen.

'Hi, you.'

'Hi, Saskia. How did today go?'

'It was fantastic,' I told him. 'I have an autographed copy of *Nun Tales* for Sophie. I got one for Athena too.'

'Thank you, Saskia, that's so thoughtful of you.'

'Thank you for the food,' I gushed, 'Everyone was raving about it so I made sure to plug the deli.'

'Thank you, and it was no problem. I'm glad I could help.'

We said goodnight and I settled on a new crime thriller, managing two episodes before I fell asleep, leaving the TV playing to itself.

Friday night had arrived, bringing our dinner party with it.

Beth, Matt and I were all feeling anxious as Ben, Stacey and Jim were all coming for food tonight so it had to go smoothly.

'I hope everyone gets on tonight,' Beth said, nervously.

'I think they will,' I said thoughtfully. 'I just hope the food goes down well,' I added.

'My food is always great,' Matt boasted.

'Yes, but Jim is a qualified chef!' Beth laughed, poking him in the ribs.

Matt's smile turned to worry.

'I'm sure your food will be great,' I said, 'It's dessert I'm worried about.'

We had taken a course each; Beth had opted for starters as her nachos were second to none and Matt was preparing his perfect steak for mains, leaving me with dessert.

It was what I excelled at and I was going with a chocolate fudge cake made from scratch.

I weighed out the ingredients meticulously, then switched the mixer to top speed. Beth and I belted out Christina Aguilera for Matt's entertainment as I carefully placed the cake tins into the oven and closed the door, staring at them through the glass.

While they cooked, we cleared away the dishes and wiped flecks of cake batter from the work surfaces. I was transported back in time to my mum teaching me how to bake when I was a teenager and letting me into her secret that making mess was an important part of the process.

The three of us navigated the kitchen well, with the odd

apology when getting in the way.

Beth's nachos were layered and covered with salsa and cheese, waiting to go in the oven.

Once the cake had cooled, I slathered on the chocolate topping and added some small chunks of fudge for good measure.

I admired my creation, then remembered who I was cooking for and my nerves returned.

Matt had prepped his homemade chips, which were now ready to go in the air fryer. The steaks lay on the chopping board, resting before being seasoned.

We had prepared all we could, so went to change and freshen up.

Then the doorbell rang and Beth answered the door to Ben, who reached up to kiss her on the lips, taking her into his arms. I couldn't help but smile at them; these pair were meant for each other.

Before the door could close, Stacey then Jim arrived in quick succession.

Stacey was very quiet at first, sitting at Matt's side silently until spoken to.

We introduced everyone and filed through into the kitchen to take our seats at the table.

'It's lovely to finally meet you, Stacey,' I said, smiling at her.

'Yes,' Beth added. 'It's taken him long enough to introduce us.' She laughed.

'It's nice to meet you both too,' she said nervously.

We did our best to make her feel comfortable and include her in every conversation and, quite quickly, she warmed up to us.

She had short blonde hair and pixie-like features, reminding me of Tinkerbell. Matt was clearly completely smitten with her.

The guys all seemed to hit it off quickly and were soon discussing the latest football scores.

Everyone got on so well and the conversation flowed as easily as the wine, over all three courses which were a complete hit.

And getting to know Ben a bit more was good; to see who my best friend was spending all her time with – I could definitely see the attraction. But, try as I might, my mind wouldn't stay on much for long before it wandered back to Jim.

I couldn't help feeling more towards him than I would care to admit. It had only been a few weeks but already I felt closer to him than I had any other guy before. I had never felt this comfortable with a partner. I was always trying to be someone different in order to be accepted. But Jim seemed to appreciate all the things I saw as flaws. My awkwardness didn't embarrass him like it had my previous boyfriends.

Before, I always felt as if I was being settled for, but the way Jim looked at me made me feel like the most beautiful person in the world.

Once we had finished eating, our three guests helped to clear away the plates and load the dishwasher, refusing to let us do it alone.

The six of us made quick work of it and were soon back at the table opening another bottle of wine.

At the end of the night, Beth, who was a little worse for wear, went home with Ben. Matt had invited Stacey to stay at ours, so when Jim asked if I would like to go home with him, I couldn't resist, telling Matt with a wink that he could have the house to himself, feeling quite drunk myself from the copious amounts of wine and the fantastic company.

He took me straight upstairs and into his room where I laid on the bed. He disappeared and returned a few minutes later with mugs of tea for us both.

'So, Mr Edwards, how was dinner?' I quizzed him.

'Very impressive,' he replied. 'And your friends are great. I'm ready for more dessert though!'

I loved the sparkle in his eyes whenever he felt naughty.

'Well, I'm glad to hear that, because I have more in store for you,' I said with a smile.

'Your turn for the cuffs.'

He looked perplexed. 'Oh, uh, I've never been tied up before.' He stammered slightly.

'Oh, really? Then maybe just your hands,' I suggested, hoping he would comply.

'Uh, yes. OK,' he said, not sounding too confident.

Ignoring his nerves, I pulled the cuffs from under his mattress, laid him on his back with his head raised up on the pillows and secured both his hands at shoulder height.

'It's about time I was in charge,' I whispered in his ear, gently biting on his ear lobe.

I undid his shirt, revealing his abs and stomach, flecked with dark hairs, then walked across the room and stood where he had a good view.

I slowly removed every item of my clothing, standing naked and feeling butterflies fluttering around my stomach. I stretched my arms up, then ran my hands down my sides, reaching back up to cup my breasts.

As I rolled my nipples between my finger and thumb, I saw his jeans begin to rise. I tiptoed my fingers down my stomach and slowly circled my clit. He watched intently, barely blinking as I pushed my fingers inside myself, groaning quietly as I brought myself to my well-rehearsed finish.

I sauntered back over to the bed where he lay licking his lips, eagerly waiting for my company and put my fingers to his mouth. He slowly sucked on one as I straddled him, moving up until my knees were either side of his face. He looked up in delight and tried to reach me, but couldn't quite get there. I let him stare for a little while, enjoying his voyeurism, then gently lowered myself onto his mouth.

His tongue instantly sprang to life, delving straight inside me, as if he had been starved of this for weeks. Looking down was a beautiful sight; seeing his head between my thighs and the look of pure contentment on his face brought me closer to my goal.

His hands still tied and pulling against the restraints, I was leading. Grinding my pussy against his face, speeding up and leaning back, I screamed out. The pleasure was too much to take as I came hard and he lapped it up.

Seconds later, I was ready for more, feeling thankful for multiple orgasms.

I pulled at his jeans, swiftly removing his boxers at the same time, and watched his cock bounce up to meet me.

I lowered my mouth onto him, feeling him twitch and buck against me. As I took him deep and gripped his shaft with one hand, I felt his balls tighten as he came close.

I stopped sucking and gently licked the head, slowing him down, then sat up.

'I need to be inside you!' he growled.

Not needing to be asked twice, I expertly ripped the wrapper off a condom from the bedside drawer, rolled it on, then sat down on his cock, pushing him up inside me, still dripping from the good work his mouth had done.

Sitting up and leaning back to give him a good view, I bounced up and down, moaning and breathing heavily. Ready to come again, my fingers found my clit once more and his face twisted into what looked like pure ecstasy as he watched me bring myself to orgasm with the use of his cock buried deep inside me.

As I came, so did he, the pulsing of his dick furthering my pleasure.

I lay on his chest for a while until he broke the silence. 'Fuck, Sass!'

I smiled, not needing any more words from him. I uncuffed him, deciding it should not be the last time he was restrained.

Chapter 7

The bedroom door opened, waking me, and as I rubbed my eyes sleepily, I saw Jim walking over to the bed with a tray.

'You looked too beautiful to wake first thing, so I made bacon sandwiches and coffee,' he said, sliding back into bed beside me.

'You're a keeper, James Edwards.' I smiled, picking up my sandwich. We had used a lot of energy up last night and I was famished.

Jim was dressed in grey joggers. The waistband, loosely hanging around his hips, showed off those beautiful abs.

As I was thinking about a sleepy morning session, I rolled over and picked up my phone from the bedside table.

'Ah crap, I'd better get the shop opened up,' I said, pulling a grumpy face when I saw the time.

I showered and dressed in the clothes I had packed the previous night, then we walked into work together, with a lingering kiss on the doorstep of the deli.

The day flew by as I was texting Jim for the most of it. It was very full-on, and I worried about how fast we were moving, but I constantly talked myself down, deciding not to rock the boat. I had never had a relationship like it, maybe that meant it was real.

As I walked up the path to the house, my phone rang. It

was Jim.

'Hey, Saskia. I just wanted to let you know I have been invited with a plus one to a charity event next weekend.

It's a few hours' drive away in a really fancy hotel. I would love you to join me.'

My heart flipped a little. He wants to take me to a charity event. In a fancy hotel.

'I would love to go,' I said, beaming down the phone. 'Who is hosting the event?'

Jim paused for a brief moment. 'Julia, she's on my mum's side of the family and I said we would go early in the day and help set up.'

'Absolutely, that sounds great, I just need to get some cover for the shop and—' I stopped.

'What's the matter?'

'I have arranged to visit my parents the evening before to stay the night and spend the day with them. But I can meet you there for the evening, how far away would it be from my parents?'

'It's just over an hour from Exeter.' he said. 'I would really love you to be there.'

'That's great, then,' I said, back at full excitement. 'I will be there.'

I got up Sunday morning and went straight to the gym, getting a good hour and a half in before a swim. I had neglected my body recently, in the sense of working out, but felt it had been awoken in the bedroom.

I had never enjoyed sex quite so much, but Jim had me listening to my body. It was as if he understood what I wanted better than I did.

Matt and I spent a lot of Sunday afternoon lounging on the sofa watching trashy TV and making Sunday dinner between us. It was a nice change from the hectic lives we had both been living recently.

For the following week, work came and went with a definite increase in customers.

Emily had helped more than she knew and I was so grateful, I dropped her an email to thank her.

The summer was always great for customers, but, during the colder months, it was so hard to get people through the door.

There were a handful of regulars who were very loyal, but, in a small coastal town, there's only so much marketing you can do.

Beth, Matt and I had spent hours brainstorming and coming up with great ideas, but even the ones that initially appeared successful soon fizzled out.

This was my dream, but it was a constant worry trying to pay the overheads and make ends meet.

Beth was sending outfit ideas for the charity event via text. Some from her own wardrobe and some she had found online.

We need a shopping trip, Miss Matthews!

How about Wednesday after work? That should give us enough time to figure something else out if we come home empty-handed.

Perfect

This was time we apparently didn't need. In the fourth shop we went into, Beth called from the other side of a rack, 'I've found it. This is the one!'

I went into the changing room with the red dress over my arm. It was almost floor-length, with a split on one side to the thigh. I put it on and was surprised by how good it looked. I stepped out and Beth did a slow clap, accompanied by a wolf whistle.

'That looks stunning on you!' she said, beaming. 'Oh, and I have the perfect heels for it too!' she practically squealed.

After a very productive shopping trip, we grabbed a ready-cooked chicken, some pasta and garlic bread from the local supermarket and headed home to cook.

Thursday evening we had a little fashion show, completing the outfit with Beth's heels – which were indeed perfect – and found jewellery and a bag to add to it. Happy with the outfit, we said goodnight and went to bed. I promised Beth I would keep her updated about how it was going as I wouldn't see her until after the event.

Friday felt long and dragged a lot. I pottered about the shop and spent over an hour at my computer, advertising on all the shop social media sites. My lunchtime trip to the deli helped, even though we never had time for anything more than quick pleasantries as Jim made my salad.

I stood at the front of the queue smiling at my beautiful man.

'Hey you,' I said, still unable to believe that he was mine.

'Hi, beautiful.' He greeted me with a smile as big as my own.

'How is your day going?' I asked, getting my card out to pay for my lunch.

'All the better for seeing you,' he said, putting his hand over mine and pushing my card away gently. 'On the house.' He grinned.

'Perks of sleeping with the boss?' I asked quietly.

'Of course,' he said, laughing softly.

'I'm looking forward to tomorrow.'

'Me too. What time are you leaving for your parents?'

'I'm going to close the shop in about an hour, grab my stuff and will be leaving then.'

'Drive safe, and let me know when you arrive, please?' he said, looking serious now.

'Of course,' I said as I leaned forward to give him a quick peck before taking my lunch and leaving him to the lunch rush.

Once I had closed the shop, I rushed home to grab my bags, packing the last few essentials. I checked my tyres and water, then got on the road.

A couple of hours later, I pulled into the drive of my childhood home.

As I got out of the car and walked around to the boot I heard my little sister screaming 'Saskia!'

As Athena ran down to meet me, I grabbed her and pulled her into a huge hug. At twelve years old, I was still her favourite person and I hadn't seen her for around two months, though we often Facetimed to keep in touch. She was such a sweet girl and I was so proud of the young woman she growing up to be.

My parents were now walking to the car, both squeezing me tightly. My dad took my case in as my mum pushed me back to arms' length to look at me. 'I've missed you so much, my darling,' she said, pulling me back into her arms. The familiar scent of her perfume took me to my happy place.

Walking back into my childhood home always felt the same. Pure bliss. This home had always been such a happy one and still was.

Nothing seemed to change there, even though the walls had been refreshed since I visited last. It still smelled the same. Not a particular smell, or one I could describe. Just one that made me breathe it in deeply and smile.

We had a fantastic evening, catching up on everything we had missed. Athena told me all about her friends and how school was going. Mum and Dad filled me in on what had been happening in work. They were both nearing retirement age now so were winding down their working lives.

They demanded I tell them everything about the book signing, how Matt and Beth were, life in general and, more importantly, Jim.

Obviously I left out one part of our relationship, but, as I told them about how sweet he was, I could feel myself grinning. My mum gave me a knowing smile and told me how pleased it made her to see me this happy.

I showed Athena my new dress and she approved. 'You are going to look like a princess.' She grinned at me.

Athena's room was that of a typical teenage girl. I smiled as I looked around her room at little trinkets from our holidays and pictures of her and her friends grinning wildly and sticking out their tongues for the camera.

There was an almost life-sized poster of Shawn Mendez. I laughed, remembering Westlife covering my walls as a teenager.

'You want to help me get ready?' I asked.

'Can I? Really?' she squealed.

'Of course,' I said, kissing her on the forehead.

'Good night, Athy,' I said, switching her light off.

'Good night, Sass.'

My old bedroom brought back so many memories. Nights of lying on my bed laughing down the phone to a friend or crying over some boy.

Sleepovers where no sleep ever took place, just midnight snacking and ghost stories by torchlight.

Reminiscing, I finally drifted off to sleep. My dreams were a mixture of school friends and Jim.

Walking around corridors with Jim at my side, then school disappearing around me and having school friends sat in the shop.

Chapter 8

I woke confused the next morning, briefly forgetting where I was.

I was so looking forward to spending the day with my family, then, to top it off, had a posh night out with my man.

I picked up my phone to see a message from him.

Good morning beautiful, how was your evening?

I responded. *Good morning. It was lovely thank you. I can't wait to see you tonight.*

My parents and Athena had planned a lovely day, starting with a hearty breakfast; as my mum always said, it's the most important meal of the day.

We had a picnic in the local park and the weather was beautiful. Summer was definitely on its way.

'Can I have some cider?' Athena asked with a grin on her face.

Mum eyed her suspiciously.

'Just a taste,' she begged. 'I tasted it before and liked it. Remember, when Saskia was here last time?'

'Hey, don't go blaming me!' I said, laughing.

She looked back at Mum, pleading with her eyes.

'Just a little taste then.' She agreed, watching her as she picked up the bottle of my strawberry and lime Koppaberg.

"Mmmmm," she said, handing it back with a smile.

“That’s what I was worried about,” Mum said, shaking her head and laughing.

We sat in the sun, watching the world go by and enjoying the rare time together.

After our lunch we visited some family and friends, laughing the day away.

True to my word, once I was out of the shower and wrapped in my robe, I called Athena in and she sat with me while I did my hair and makeup. Giving pointers and ideas. At her age I didn’t have a clue about these things, but she was good, showing how different youngsters were today. Ready to go, I walked downstairs. My parents were waiting at the bottom, smiles plastered over their faces and taking pictures as if I was on my way to the prom.

‘I hope Jim knows how lucky he is,’ my dad said, squeezing my shoulder.

‘And do bring him to meet us soon,’ added my mum. ‘We will behave, we promise.’

‘Of course I will,’ I assured them. ‘I will be back up as soon as I can, and I will bring Jim with me.‘

I hugged them all one by one. I know how much my mum hated being so far away, but would never tell me so.

I remember the first letter she sent me when I moved away. There was a little card in the envelope, the size of a credit card. It said...

We give our children but two things..

The first is roots, the second is wings.

I still carried it in my purse, always making me feel closer to her.

We said our goodbyes and my dad loaded my case back

into the car.

I put the hotel postcode into the sat nav and my nerves kicked in. I had never been to anything like this on my own before. I hoped that I would be able to find Jim quickly so had sent him a text just before leaving

Hi, I'm just about to leave. Where will I find you when I get there? x

I received an instant reply.

I'll meet you in the main hall x

My family waved until they were out of sight and I flicked the radio on to keep me company for the journey, singing at the top of my voice to every song I knew the words to. As I pulled into the hotel car park, I noticed the valet parking and did a quick scan of the car, shoving the CDs from the seat into the glove box and squeezing an empty water bottle into the door.

I exchanged my car keys for a ticket and checked my reflection in the little mirror from my handbag, reapplying some lipstick and ascending the stairs, praying I wouldn't trip.

The reception area was mesmerizing to an almost intimidating level. The space was impressive and looked so high class and fancy. Shiny white tiles donned the floors and my heels click-clacked as I walked across them. There was a huge marble desk to the side, where a blonde lady stood, greeting the guests with a smile. Her long hair fell in waves around her petite shoulders. She wore a very expensive-looking suit jacket over a fitted white shirt and her bright-red lips parted to show bright-white teeth. I smiled at her as I walked past, trying hard to look comfortable. This couldn't be further from the truth. I was so far out of my comfort zone and desperate to find Jim.

I found the main hall and awkwardly wandered around to the bar area, searching for Jim but unable to see him. A waitress came over with a tray of champagne, offering me a glass. I thanked her and took one, hands trembling a little with the nerves.

The room was beautiful. Decorated to perfection and alive with the hum of rich people dressed to the nines.

I breathed a sigh of relief that I had gone with Beth's outfit choice. It fitted in nicely with the dress code.

I felt him enter the crowded room and watched as he scanned the room before finding me.

He was dressed in a tailored black suit, white shirt and bowtie and just looking at him made my knees weak. Staring at me with the look that only I knew, he walked through the room and past me without a second glance and headed into the corridor.

I waited for a moment, unsure what just happened, then followed him out.

He met me in the corridor, and, his hand lightly on my back, ushered me into the lift.

As soon as the doors closed, he pushed me up against the mirrored walls.

Before I knew what was happening, he had my dress pulled up and my thong around my knees.

Roughly pulling my legs apart, he put his fingers inside me.

He covered my mouth as I started to moan.

Then, as quickly as it happened, I was dressed again and desperate for more as the lift doors opened.

I caught sight of my flustered face in the mirrors as we exited the lift, passing a few people waiting to get in.

We get to a room and he opens the door with a key card and directs me in.

'That dress,' he mutters, shaking his head in approval.

He watches as I slip it off, along with my underwear, draping it carefully over the back of a chair.

He pushes me onto the bed, undoes his fly and frees his straining cock.

Without an invitation, I have my mouth on him, sucking him in deeper.

I'm gagging on his length, but still I want more.

I let him take the control and look up at him while he fucks my mouth.

Close to cumming, he pulls away.

It must be my turn now, and I can't wait to feel his mouth on me.

He pulls me to sit up and he lies on the bed, still fully clothed.

He guides me on top until I'm straddling his face, then, gripping my arse, pulls me into his mouth.

I lean back as he glides his hands up to my tits and pulls at my nipples while I ride his mouth.

Shaking with pleasure, I cum all over his face.

He pulls on a condom, turns me round to face away from him and lifts me back on top while easing his cock inside me. Kneeling up, I lean forward until I'm lying on his legs so he can watch as he fucks me.

I love to know he's watching.

Slowly at first, he slides in and out, savouring each moment. I can't take the teasing anymore and start to rock backwards onto him; he matches my rhythm and starts pounding into me. Feeling his cock pulsing as he cums inside me brings me to another climax.

I slump down onto his legs and he gives my arse a sharp slap.

Having barely uttered two words to me, he now turns to me, telling me how beautiful I look. 'Sorry, Sass, as soon as I saw you, I needed to have you.' The words make my tingle again.

Checking my hair and makeup in the mirror, I don't need to reapply my lipstick; my lips are red and swollen from his mouth.

He straightens his shirt, puts on his jacket and we go downstairs to re-join the party.

As soon as we enter the main room, a beautiful girl with dark hair and eyes comes over to us.

'Saskia, this is Julia, Julia, this is Saskia,' says Jim, wrapping his arm around my waist.

'I've heard so much about you.' Julia smiles warmly.

'Ah, nothing bad, I hope,' I said.

'What an amazing job you have done, it all looks fantastic.'

Julia grinned at me. 'Thank you so much. It's been hard work, but I've had a lot of help.'

'I'm going to get us some drinks while you ladies get acquainted,' Jim announced, my waist suddenly feeling cold without his arm.

Julia grins at me as he moves away. 'He would kill me if he knew, but, I have to tell you, Saskia, I have never seen him so happy.'

I feel the start of a blush. 'You really think so?' I stutter, kicking myself for sounding like a high school girl with a crush.

'Jim has never really had much of a relationship, not that there haven't been any, but he has never really introduced us to anyone; has always said there was no one special in his life. But you... You're all he talks about.'

Finding myself grinning as much as Julia, I let my guard down a little.

'We haven't been together that long, but, honestly, I am so happy. It's nice to know he is too,' I told her, unable to remove the grin from my face.

Jim arrives back at my side with drinks and Julia thanks him, takes her glass and then excuses herself to go and mingle with her guests, touching Jim's arm and gently squeezing before turning to face me.

'It was really lovely to meet you, Saskia, thank you both so much for being here this evening. It means a lot.'

'Likewise,' I say, honestly. 'Thank you so much for inviting me.'

I spotted Jim's parents from a mile off. He couldn't look more like his dad if he tried, and he had his mother's mannerisms.

His dad looked as though he was born in a suit. I would place him around mid-fifties and he oozed an easy-going confidence with greying hair and a slim build. His eyes were dark, just like Jim's, and he had aged well.

His mum, who looked maybe a year or two younger, was dressed beautifully in a silver, floor-length gown and had a calmness about her. She was very softly spoken and wore a happy smile.

Such lovely people, and so well-to-do. It was easy to see why Jim was so well spoken and, also, where his other lovely traits came from.

Even though I was surrounded by wealthy people, they didn't once make me feel out of place.

Having grown up in such a different setting, the only parties I was used to generally ended up with my aunts and uncles getting wasted and blasting out Tina Turner on the karaoke machine.

'I hope they like me,' I said, looking at Jim as we walked toward the bar.

A waitress headed in our direction with her tray of champagne. Jim nodded at me.

'Do you want something different?'

'No,' I said, a little quicker than I intended. 'Champagne is great.'

It really was. Not the cheap stuff you picked up in Tesco. This was the real deal, and I wasn't passing it up.

'Saskia, I know my parents. They love you already!'

'Phew!' I said, breathing a sigh of relief. 'Everyone is so lovely.'

Julia got up on the stage to a rapturous applause and thanked everyone for coming.

She told us all about the charity we were raising money for images passed slowly over a projector screen behind her.

Photographs of Julia and others sitting with smiley children in Africa. Still managing to be so happy even though they lived in poverty with more problems than we could ever imagine.

'Your help has made this possible,' she continued, 'and with your support tonight, we can finish building the new school. These children will finally get the education they deserve. Thank you so much. Enjoy your evening.'

She stepped down and was instantly surrounded by a group of people.

I wished I was more involved in such things and admired her courage and grace.

At the end of a very successful evening, we helped Julia tidy up, which was more fun than tidying up should be, then we joined Jim's parents, aunts and uncles and some other family and friends outside.

It was a beautiful night and there was a fire burning in a pit inside a circular bench.

The flames licked at the logs in the fire pit, the smoke rising up in to the sky and disappearing among the stars. The heat radiating out warmed me through.

Julia came out and sat next to Jim with a long sigh.

'You did it, Jules,' he said, patting her leg.

'Ah, thank you, Jim, couldn't have managed it without you.' She grinned. 'You have been a life-saver today. Putting out fires all over the place.' She laughed, touching his arm again. He looked down at her hand and she pulled it away quickly.

'You did a marvellous job, Julia.' Jim's mum announced. 'We are all very proud of you.'

'Thank you, Margaret.' Julia smiled warmly.

'Margaret, my dear,' Jim's dad said, standing up. 'I think it is time for us oldies to get some rest.' He stretched, then tucked his shirt back into his suit trousers.

He was a lot like Jim in many ways, very polite and sweet; you could definitely see the family resemblance.

He offered his hand to Margaret and she took it, gracefully standing up in her beautiful floor- length gown.

'Thank you, Charles,' she said. 'Good night, all, it has been a beautiful evening. Well done again, Julia,' she said, squeezing her hand and leaning down to kiss her on the cheek.

'It was an absolute pleasure to meet you, Saskia,' she said, turning to me.

I stood up and got a kiss on the cheek too.

Charles shook my hand.

'Most definitely,' he said. Then, looking at Jim, he continued, 'What a lovely young lady.'

'It was a pleasure to meet you both,' I replied and squeezed Jim's hand.

Before long, the rest of the group started to disperse until there were only the two of us left.

I lay back with my head in his lap and looked up to find him staring down at me.

I don't know if it was the wine or the just in the moment, but I felt so much for this man.

Already I couldn't bear to lose him.

'I feel like you know me so well, Jim, better than I know myself sometimes,' I said, gazing up at him.

'I know exactly what you mean, Sass. I feel the same.'

'You don't think it's going too fast, do you?' I asked, petrified of his answer.

He looked thoughtful and, for a moment, I thought my world was about to come crashing down.

'Truthfully, I have wondered the same. But I keep coming to the same answer...no. It just feels right.'

I exhaled, realising I had been holding my breath and he leaned down and kissed my head.

'It does, doesn't it?'

'You have awoken a new woman in me, you know?'

He smiled, that sparkle teasing his eyes.

'Have I now? How so?'

'Well, there are things I'd never even given much thought to, and you have shown me how much I enjoy them,' I said, coyly.

'There is so much more to explore, Sass, so much I think you would love.'

'I want you to show me!' I said brazenly. 'I want to do it all!'

Jim sat up a little. 'Any boundaries?' he asked, looking quite serious now.

I felt a thrill run down between my legs at the prospect of new experiences with him.

'I don't think so, but can I get back to you?' I giggled a little.

'Take all the time you need, Saskia. I would never push you into anything.'

He brushed the hair from my face and leaned down, putting his lips on mine.

My body practically hummed in response to him, my tongue twirling with his.

I sat up and onto his lap, pulling my dress up around my waist, extending our kiss.

He ran his hands over my breasts and up to the nape of my neck, kissing me deeper.

I reached down and undid his suit trousers, delighted to find he wasn't wearing underwear.

He stopped kissing me. 'I don't have any protection,' he said, looking disappointed.

'You do know I'm on the pill right?' I laughed. 'It's fine.'

'Are you sure?'

In answer to his question, I pulled my thong to one side and slid down onto him slowly. It was surprising how much better it felt without the thin layer of latex between us.

The fire still burned in the pit and was now the only light, casting shadows on our bodies as we became one.

This time was different; it was slow and passionate rather

than the rampant fuck we usually shared.

He kissed my neck as I leaned my head back, rubbing my clit against him as I sat down, taking him in deeper each time.

I felt his hot, sticky cum pump inside me as I climaxed, squeezing around him.

He called out my name as he emptied himself into me, then pulled me tighter against his chest.

We sat there briefly, as we both recovered, then messily made our way up to the room.

The bedroom was beautiful, I hadn't had chance to notice earlier.

A huge four-poster bed was the main focus. There was a beautiful wardrobe with matching dresser off to the side and a large TV filled most of the wall opposite the bed. Next to the dresser there was a tea and coffee station, but not like you would find at a Travelodge; it was a full-blown percolator, with fancy cups on saucers and more tea choices than I even knew existed.

Realising I hadn't cleaned myself up after our outside excursion, I went straight into the bathroom. It was almost as nice as Jim's at home. When I emerged in the pyjama bottoms and vest top I'd packed, Jim was lying down. He patted the bed next to him.

I slid under the cool, crisp sheets and cuddled into him.

He stroked my hair and told me how much he had enjoyed the evening and how happy he was. I was about to agree with him and thank him for such a lovely time when he said it,

'I love you, Saskia.'

It took me by surprise at first, rendering me speechless.

'I know we haven't been together long and maybe it is a bit fast, but it's how I feel and I felt I should tell you,' he finished, sounding very calm and contented.

He didn't seem to need a response from me, but, as I lay there, my mind recounted all the times I had felt the same.

'I love you too.'

He smiled and squeezed me tighter.

He loves me, and I love him. This could be it. I had never felt this way about anyone before and had searched for 'the real thing' for so long. I was doing a happy little dance in my head.

I glanced at the clock, suddenly exhausted.

'It's gone four!' I said, quite shocked that I'd made it up this late.

'Time for some sleep.' He chuckled. 'Goodnight, beautiful.'

'Goodnight, you,' I replied, before falling into a happy, dreamless sleep, wrapped in the arms of my love.

Chapter 9

I woke the next morning in the third room in as many days. Jim was awake next to me, smiling as I turned to him.

He leaned forward and kissed me, pulling me on top of him.

'Well good morning, Mr Edwards,' I said, sitting up and pushing my naked breasts into his face.

'Good morning to you,' he replied, in between sucking on my nipple.

The feeling sent instant waves between my legs and I let out a quiet moan.

He pushed his erection up against me and I pushed down on him, rubbing myself on him through my knickers.

'These need to go,' he told me, pulling them off my feet.

I rubbed on him again, the feeling of his skin on my clit immense.

Grinding myself against him, he moaned and gripped me tightly around the waist.

Just as I was about to climax, he pulled back slightly and thrust up inside me.

'Jim!' I cried out, cumming hard.

He continued after my orgasm. I felt like I needed to stop for a moment, but I know all too well that if anyone knows what I need, it's Jim.

He sped up as I bounced around on top of him, pushing me

down onto his throbbing cock.

He had found my G-spot and was hammering against it.

He moaned as he came, spurring my next along with it.

The feeling of no condom was still very new and I loved how it felt. Judging by his face, so did he.

After a shower, we were in the dining area, sat at a closely placed rectangular tables.

There were crisp white table clothes and bone-china tea cups on saucers, so delicate I wasn't sure I trusted myself with one.

Waiters, dressed in penguin suits, served us whatever type of breakfast we wanted.

There was Full English with copious amounts of hot buttered toast, cereals, pastries, every fruit imaginable and continental with fresh bread and meats.

Unable to make a decision just yet, I allowed the waiter to top up my tea cup and also fill a glass with orange juice.

Jim slid into the seat next to me and patted my leg.

'Well this looks nice, doesn't it?'

'It really does, I can't decide what to have,' I said, still struggling with the decision I was facing.

'Full English for me, please,' he said to the waiter who smiled sweetly at me, looking for an answer.

'Um... I will go with the continental, please,' I stuttered, instantly changing my mind, but deciding it was too late.

'Of course,' he said, bowing slightly and leaving the table.

'What a fantastic night it was,' said one of the older ladies at a nearby table.

'It really was,' Jim's mum responded. 'Julia did herself proud.'

‘It is so heart-warming to know that this has helped those darling little children,’ the lady said, clasping her hands to her heart.

I nodded along, trying my hardest to remember who the lady was.

Julia appeared at the doorway, looking almost as glamorous as she did last night in a pale-lemon summer dress.

She waved at us and made her way over.

‘Good morning, everyone.’ She smiled. ‘Jim, would you be a darling and give me a hand with something?’

Jim jumped up and looked back at me. ‘Won’t be a minute,’ he said as he walked off.

I watched them disappear out of the dining room.

Jim’s mum glanced up at Julia, but the dining room continued to bustle with the waiters gliding seamlessly between the tables, placing plates and drinks in front of the guests.

The walls were cream with bold chocolate-brown thick stripes and low-hanging lamp shades just above the tables.

I was left with a lady I had been introduced to as Auntie Caroline, and her husband Uncle Tom.

‘So is Julia your daughter?’ I asked, suddenly realising that I actually had no idea what part of the family she was from.

‘No, dear,’ she said. ‘Just a son for me, Stephen. I think you met him last night.’

‘Ah, yes.’ I nodded, still none the wiser.

‘Julia isn’t any blood relation to the family, just a very good family friend,’ she told me.

‘Her and Jim have been friends since they were children. A bit closer than friends for a while though, if you know what I mean?’ She gave me a playful dig in the ribs.

'Carol,' Tom said as a warning, but she didn't seem to hear him.

'Yes, they were quite the item those two. Talk of the town.' She smiled fondly. 'I was very surprised when they parted. Thought they were made for each other.'

'Carol!' Tom repeated, fixing her with a stare. 'Why don't we take a little walk around the garden?' he suggested, drinking the last of his tea.

'Well I haven't quite finished, dear,' she said, looking a little startled.

'I think you have,' he told her, taking her hand and leading her out of the dining room.

Made for each other! Talk of the town!

He didn't think to mention this before inviting me to her charity event!

I was seething, how could he not tell me?

Why did he think it was OK to bring me here?

How dare he make a fool of me like this?

What's more, where the fuck was he?

I couldn't just sit here, I had to get out.

As I stood to leave, the waiter brought our breakfast.

The plate of fresh breads, meats and cheeses looked divine.

I thanked him and briefly thought about eating first; I was ravenous.

Then I picked up a bread roll and walked out of the dining hall.

I stormed down the corridor to our room and swiped the key card. The red light flashed. I swiped it again; *stupid fancy hotel where the stupid key doesn't even work*, I cursed as I swiped it a third time and the green light came on.

I pushed the door open and started throwing my clothes and toiletries in my case.

I slammed the door behind me and walked back to the reception desk.

'I'd like to check out please,' I told the receptionist, placing my card on the desk.

She picked it up and scanned it into the machine. 'How was your stay?' she asked politely.

'Yes, lovely, thank you.' I tried to stay calm. After all, it wasn't her fault that my boyfriend had brought me here for a fancy night out with his ex. An ex his auntie clearly wanted back in his life.

I left the reception desk and walked out into the driveway, realising that I had no idea where my car was – or the keys, for that matter.

Storming back into the hotel, I went back to the desk looking like an idiot.

'Um, my car,' I started. 'The valet parked it yesterday.'

'Of course.' She smiled. 'Do you have your ticket?'

Ticket, where was my ticket?

I dumped my handbag onto the desk and started rooting through it.

'Saskia, what's the matter?' came Jim's voice from across the entrance hall.

I closed my eyes and took a deep breath.

I looked back at the lady; she clearly sympathised with me, but couldn't go giving my car to just anyone.

'Saskia!' Jim called again, right behind me this time.

Don't make a scene, I told myself under my breath.

I looked back down into my handbag and saw the little blue ticket smiling up at me.

I grabbed it and slammed it onto the counter.

'I will have them bring your car round,' the lady said, looking very uncomfortable.

I smiled at her and turned to face Jim.

'Where are you going?' he asked, looking confused.

'Well I thought you and *Julia* could do with some alone time. You know, rekindle that lost love!' I spat.

'What are you on about?' he said quietly, trying to avoid the scene I wasn't going to make.

'How could you not tell me who she was?' I demanded. 'I thought she was your cousin or something.'

'You never asked,' he said sheepishly.

'She's on my mum's side,' I said, reminding him of who he had tried to pass her off as.

He looked at me, helpless.

'Forget it! I snapped and turned to walk away.

'Please, Saskia.' He grabbed my arm.

'Don't touch me!' I shouted, pulling away and crossing the entrance hall to the front door.

He followed me outside to where my little car was waiting for me, her engine running ready for me to escape.

I fought back tears of anger and upset as I slung my case into the boot.

'Please, Saskia! I should have told you who Julia was,' he pleaded.

'You think?' I muttered, not even looking at him.

'But it was so long ago, there has been nothing between us for ten years, Sass, we are just friends. Like you and Matt.'

'The difference is,' I said, turning to look at him as I pulled the driver door open. 'I've never fucked Matt.'

I got in and slammed the door, driving off before he could open it again.

Tears streamed down my face as I navigated the streets while wiping my eyes with the sleeve of my jacket.

My phone started ringing, it was Jim. I pressed the Cancel button on the car screen and knocked the Bluetooth off, disconnecting it.

I turned the music up and drove until my stomach demanded I stop to eat.

Having drunk quite a bit last night, I really needed something to soak up the alcohol.

I tapped the sat nav button on the screen and found the nearest services.

Twenty minutes later, I sat in my car eating a McDonald's breakfast muffin and hash brown, contemplating what had happened.

Had I been too harsh? I had no reason to doubt his loyalty to me. But why would he not tell me about their past?

I walked through the front door, dropped my bag and case on the floor and slumped onto the sofa.

Snowy meowed and jumped straight up onto my lap, flicking her tail in my face and needling my legs before settling.

I was exhausted from the late night and all the crying, so allowed myself to drift off.

BANG. I woke with a jump. It was someone at the front door.

I stood up and pushed a grumpy cat to the floor, then peered through the peephole.

It was Jim, he looked a mess.

Realising I couldn't ignore him for ever, neither did I want to, I opened the door a crack.

'Saskia. I was so worried about you.'

'I'm fine,' I said, coldly.

'Can I come in? Please?'

'Fine,' I said, walking away.

'I am so sorry, Saskia, I should have told you. It just didn't seem relevant and I didn't want to upset you unnecessarily.'

Looking at him, all dishevelled and worried over me, defrosted my anger a little.

'I meant what I said last night, Saskia, I love you. I love you so much and I can't bear to see you like this.'

'You should have told me,' I said. 'You shouldn't have let me go there not knowing something like that. You made a complete fool of me,' I said, feeling my anger rise up again.

'I'm sorry.

Please forgive me.' He stepped closer to me and I could smell his aftershave and minty breath as he stared into my eyes, begging for forgiveness.

I softened some more and mulled things over in my mind. I was angry with him, but was it worth losing him over? Surely not. This man was everything to me.

'Don't you dare ever pull a stunt like that again!' I said, sternly.

He grabbed my face and kissed me. 'Never,' he said, breaking contact with my lips for a split second.

He held me close as he took my mouth with his.

I pulled away and looked at him, his eyes filled with relief.

I took his hand and led him upstairs and into my bedroom.

'I don't believe we have christened this room,' I said casually as I closed the door behind us.

He sat on my bed, surrounded by scatter cushions and pulled me into his lap.

'You are so beautiful, Saskia,' he said, kissing my head.

I pulled at his fly, freeing his dick – which was ready to go – and, pushing my underwear to one side, slowly sat down on him, my dress covering us from view.

Slowly grinding on him as I rode him, he moaned and cupped my breasts, sucking gently on my nipple.

We were both done within moments, and came with the release of all the anger and upset from that morning.

Chapter 10

I had returned home after work Monday to find Matt and Stacey sat in the garden, making the most of the afternoon sun.

'Hi, Sass,' Matt said as I stepped out into the garden.

'Hi!' I greeted them cheerily.

'How are you, Stacey?' I asked.

'I'm good, thank you,' she responded, looking a little more comfortable around me than the first time we had met.

'We thought we would make the most of the sun before it disappears again,' she said, grinning like a Cheshire cat.

'Good idea,' I said. 'It rarely stays around for long.'

Matt observed the two of us as he leant into Stacey's shoulder.

We chatted a while, then I left them together to go up to my room.

I sat on my bed and opened my laptop. I had research to do.

I wasn't sure what I was letting myself in for, but was excited about what surprises Jim might have in store for me.

I needed to know what kinds of things were out there before I could tell Jim what limits I had, if any.

There was some crazy shit out there and a lot of it made me cringe, but still I delved deeper.

Looking at pictures of grown men dressed up as babies gave me the shivers and I found out that there is even a fetish for people who are aroused by fog.

But some pictures I came across during my research had a much nicer effect on me.

Bondage was definitely up my street and I think I could safely say I would very happy to be dominated.

It was getting late when I turned the laptop off and folded the list I had made of limits. It wasn't a long list.

With only two things written down, I wondered what Jim would make of it and what other crazy stuff he might be into.

My thoughts were broken by the trill of my phone. It was Beth. We hadn't spoken properly since before the charity event; just exchanged a few messages as Beth had been called into work.

She was a data analyst and her company had some kind of emergency situation that she and her colleagues had to resolve.

'Hey,' she said cheerily.

'Hi, how is work? All sorted?'

'Ah, it's been pretty rough, but we got there,' she said, sounding like the world had just been lifted from her shoulders.

'So, tell me everything. How was it?'

'It was amazing…' I gushed. 'So much money in one place, but I didn't feel out of place at all. Everyone made me feel so welcome. I met Jim's parents and they liked me, and his entire family are lovely and…' I stopped, realising I hadn't even taken a breath and what I was about to say was pretty big news.

'And what?' Beth exclaimed. 'Why have you stopped?'

'Beth, he told me he loves me.'

There was silence for a second, then a little squeak. 'Well, what did you say? How do you feel?'

I took a deep breath and told her how I had responded and everything that followed.

I felt giddy with excitement sharing this news – I had already decided to keep the argument to myself.

I felt as though I had overreacted and I was pushing away the horrible jealous feelings that surfaced whenever I thought about it.

We chatted for half an hour before Beth said she needed to get to bed.

I kept my research to myself for now too, I had given Beth enough information for one night and I wasn't sure I wanted to share this just yet.

Jim and I hadn't planned to meet for another two days so I decided that I would text him my very short list of limits.

I typed and re-typed the message until I was happy enough to press Send...

I have given it a lot of thought and have come to my conclusion.

I don't have many limits but am also not sure what you have planned, so could also probably do with some other options from you.

1. No animal role-play. Sorry if this is something you were hoping for, but I find it a little odd.

2. No pain. I am fine with a gentle spanking, but anything more is off limits.

Thoughts, please? X

I was hoping for an instant response, but, after staring at

my phone for a few minutes, I drifted off to sleep.

I woke the next morning to Jim's response...

Well, it's nice to see you have been thinking about this.

Firstly, to your limits...not a problem on either count. Completely with you on the first. Just weird.

And the second...

wouldn't want to inflict any pain on you in any way.

With regards to what I have in store for you...

Just a few suggestions, feel free to veto any or all and also suggest your own if you wish:

1. *Toys*
2. *Voyeurism*
3. *Involving others*
4. *Bondage*
5. *Blindfold*

Take your time and please know that you can always change your mind. X

I started to read the message but was half asleep still, so decided to re-visit once I had showered and opened the shop so I could give it my full attention.

Having answered the few emails that had come in, I sat down with my coffee and opened the message from Jim again.

The first thing to jump out at me was 'involving others'. It was something that I had never done, but had always been a secret fantasy of mine. Could I do it? I would need to think that one through a bit.

I already had plenty of toys, so that wasn't an issue, nor was a blindfold or bondage. I'd enjoyed being tied up, so assumed that it would just take that further.

Onto voyeurism. I loved to be watched, Jim had already shown me that. But how far would he take it?

So many questions swam around in my head so I replied saying that I would like to ask some questions.

Instantly his response came through:

Ask away, beautiful. X

I typed a message, then hit Send before I even re-read it...

Voyeurism...who would be watching or are we watching?...Other people...unsure how I would feel with you being with anyone else. X

His response made my stomach flip. At first I thought I was disgusted by the notion, but that soon gave way to excitement as I realised I was getting wet at the thought.

Voyeurism...I was thinking very public, and both watching and being watched.

And how about if I didn't have any physical contact with anyone else...just you? X

Very public! The thought of being watched by others, lots of others, made me hotter than I wanted to admit.

And him watching me with someone else got the same reaction.

I typed out two words and hit Send. Praying I wouldn't

regret my decision.

I’m in. X

Jim replied telling me that if I ever felt uncomfortable that I just needed to tell him and it would end, no further questions asked.

I felt nervous and wasn’t sure what to do with myself. Feeling like I had just become a whole new person.

I never did things like this and was about as spontaneous as a clock. But I was filled with good anticipation. Jim always made me feel so safe and I knew I could trust him. He had me wanting to push every boundary as he awakened my body.

I called hello as I walked through the front door, but stopped in my tracks as Matt ran past me and out of the door, slamming it open against the wall, followed by Stacey who was sobbing.

At the end of the drive she grabbed his arm but he pushed it off and walked away.

Unsure what to do, I stood for a while looking out at the empty street where they had both been moments before.

I went back into the house and typed a message out to Matt...

Are you OK?

I didn’t expect an answer anytime soon, but needed him to know I was here for him.

I grabbed my gym kit and headed back out of the door. I wasn’t seeing Jim until tomorrow night so wanted to get a workout in. Hoping Matt would be home when I returned, I locked the front door and got back in my car.

I managed an hour and a half in the gym before I hit the showers. I was just towelling myself off when a gorgeous, leggy blonde sauntered into the changing rooms.

I had noticed her during my workout; I could appreciate a pretty girl when I saw one.

Now she stood with her back to me, peeling herself out of her gym kit as I had done ten minutes before. I had started my post-workout moisturising regime when I glanced up and caught her staring at me in the mirror. I looked away quickly, feeling as though I had been caught doing something I shouldn't, and she walked off towards the showers.

Feeling a new and exciting buzz working its way through me, I thought again about being watched by others and excitement bubbled up inside me. I let scenarios play out in my head while I dressed and pulled my wet hair into a bobble.

Ready to leave, I checked my phone. There was a message from Matt.

Ah, fucking women, Sass. Except you and Beth, of course. Needed to clear my head but I'm on my way home. Will see you there.

He had only sent it ten minutes ago. I grabbed my bag and headed out to my car.

I texted Matt telling him I was on my way home and would pick up food.

He responded with a gif telling me he was starving. I stopped at the local Chinese and put our order in, then went next door to the off licence and grabbed some beers while the food was cooked.

As I closed the front door behind me, I saw Matt sat at the kitchen table.

He looked sad and dishevelled and had half a mug of cold tea in front of him.

I replaced his cup with a beer and gave his shoulder a squeeze. 'Let's eat first, shall we?'

He looked at me and nodded, taking a deep breath.

We ate silently and quickly. The journey back in the car with the smell of the food had made me ravenous.

Matt finished the last mouthful of his food and pushed his plate away as if it being empty offended him.
He drained the last of his beer and sighed.

'It's over, Sass,' he said with a pained look on his face.

'What happened?' I asked, finishing the last mouthful of my food and putting my chopsticks down.

'She's been hiding stuff. Bad stuff.'

My mind starting to reel with what she could have been doing.

'Her phone was on the worktop between us and it went off. The noise made me look down. I would never go through her phone but it was just there, popped up at the top of her screen.'

'Who was it? What did it say?' I asked.

'The message, or what I could see of it,' he continued, 'Said. Hey, baby girl, what time you home tonight? Can't wait to get my hands on you and... And then it disappeared.'

He looked down at the table, hurt etched across his face.

'Did you ask her about it?' I said tentatively.

'Yes, kind of wished I hadn't. It was from Richard. Her fiancé!'

‘What?’ I almost choked on my beer. ‘Her fiancé? What the fuck is she playing at?’

‘Apparently it’s an arrangement they have. One guy clearly isn’t enough for her. But then neither are two. She is also seeing some other guy across town. He doesn’t know about me or her fiancé either.’

He hung his head in shame. ‘How could I not know, Sass? I was really falling for her.’

I got up, walked over and stood behind him, putting my arms around his shoulders and hugging him tight. I hated to see him like this. He was one of my closest friends and was always there for me.

‘What a bitch! Whatever crazy arrangement her and her fiancé have, how could she not consult you and this other guy, whoever he is. Who does she think she is?’

God help anyone who hurt my friends; I was gunning for the whore.

‘Gimme your phone, I’m calling her!’ I spat out, anger flowing through me.

‘No, Sass, I’ve told her how I feel. There is nothing more to say. I’m just gonna need a bit of time.’ He said it quietly, no anger at all. He looked exhausted.

I opened another beer and passed it to him. He clinked it with mine, then put his arm around my shoulders and we walked into the front room, sitting down to watch trashy TV.

‘Thanks for always being here, Sass,’ he said as I flicked through the channels.

‘Always,’ I said, giving his arm a squeeze.

Chapter 11

It was Tuesday morning. It was the kind of Tuesday morning that made you feel sure it was Monday. The kind of Tuesday where every minute felt like an hour.

It had been very quiet in the shop today, which wasn't helping. I walked around, looking at all the books of the shelves, all the love and hard work that had gone into this place. Every little detail agonised over.

I worried a lot about the shop. But that's what having your own business is, I suppose. The beauty of being your own boss and making your own rules; however, those perks also come with a lot of weight to bear.

Although I had plenty of help to get up and running, this business was mine; therefore, if it failed, it would be my failure.

I snapped myself out of the slump I was falling into. I was seeing Jim tonight and I couldn't wait.

Telling someone you love them for the first time then having your first fight within twelve hours can really shake things up.

I felt as though we were closer than ever and was excited about the new things he might have in store.

We were meeting for dinner at the local pub and I hoped we would end up back at his.

At 12 p.m. I put the sign in the window, locked the door and wandered round to the deli.

Jim was looking gorgeous as always.

I watched him for a while before I went in, stealing some moments for myself.

He wiped his brow with his upper arm as he washed his hands and pulled on fresh gloves.

It was warm today and although the deli was beautifully air-conditioned, he was so busy that he was working up a sweat.

'You could do with some help in here, Jim,' I said as I got to the counter.

'Hey, beautiful, you're in early today.' He beamed at me. His dark hair, although short on the sides, was getting quite long on the top and had started to fall into his eyes, giving him a mischievous look.

'Hi, my morning has gone about as quickly as the rush hour traffic,' I said, rolling my eyes.

'I couldn't wait any longer to see your face.' I smiled.

'Well seeing your face always makes my day,' he told me with a gorgeous smile, turning my insides to mush.

'Are we still meeting at eight?' I asked, trying to act nonchalant.

'Yes. Eight is perfect. I'm looking forward to it.'

Feeling happy, I left him with a shop of hungry customers.

As I screwed up my lunch bag, the shop phone rang. It was a man from the careers department. He asked me to speak at a careers day for the local high school.

I told him that I would be honoured and would just need to check I could get cover for the shop that day and would confirm by the end of the week.

Before I knew it, the rest of the afternoon had passed and I was locking the front door again.

The house was now empty and I went upstairs to get changed. In a mint-green wrap dress and a pair of heeled sandals, I left the house.

As I walked into the pub, I saw Jim stand up at a table to greet me. We chatted about our days and I told Jim I was going to speak at the high school next week.

We had a lovely homemade curry and rice and washed it down with a beer. I had been worrying about how he would be around me; having confessed love for each other last time we were together.

I shouldn't have worried; everything was just the same, except it all felt even more comfortable and easy.

'So, I have a surprise for our next date,' he announced. 'Something new to try, if you're free Saturday night?'

Excitement rippled through me. This was it. Our first in, hopefully, a long line of new things to explore.

'That sounds exciting,' I told him, grinning.

'Come to mine straight from work, you can shower there if you like?' Jim suggested, with an easy-going smile; a smile that reached his dark eyes. I let my gaze roam over his perfect jaw line to his full lips, surrounded by his neatly trimmed stubble.

'Sounds great.'

Once Jim had paid the bill, we went outside and stood by his truck.

He gently brushed the hair from my face and tucked it behind my ear.

Those big brown eyes stared directly into my soul. 'You want to come back to mine?'

'I thought you'd never ask,' I teased.

He leaned in and his lips touched mine, his tongue slowly making its way into my mouth.

We stood like that for what felt like hours; my body craved him so badly, and, with his erection pressed against my hip, he clearly wanted me too.

He finally pulled away and kissed the tip of my nose.

'Come on, you' he said, opening the door for me.

We got back to his and he poured us both a glass of wine.

We took them into the bedroom and sat side by side, sipping the full-bodied red.

I had only managed a few sips from my glass when he took it from my hand and placed it next to his on the bedside table.

He leaned in and kissed me, then rolled me on to my front, supporting himself above my legs.

He ran his hands up the backs of my thighs and to my bum, alternating between massaging and lightly tracing his fingers over me.

He leaned over and gathered my hair, pushing it over my shoulder. I felt his hot breath on my skin as his lips gently grazed my neck, sending waves of pleasure directly to my core.

He kissed along my neck and down my back; each time he did, another gasp escaped my lips.

My entire body felt as though an electric current was running through it.

I felt him lay down on me as he penetrated me easily; sliding in as he continued to plant his electric kisses on me.

My back involuntarily arched as he affected every inch of me.

Just as my orgasm began to build, he pulled out and turned me over.

'I want to look at you,' he growled.

I moaned at his words and laid on my back, opening my legs for him.

He gazed at me for a moment, then put his mouth on me.

I gasped at the sudden pleasure and was so close to cumming for him.

He sat up and left me lying there, legs splayed.

I was desperate for his touch, and, when he didn't oblige, I rolled onto my side, wrapping my legs around him and humping myself against his thigh.

He watched me as I brought myself to a finish.

'That face,' he said darkly. 'Fuck, I love to watch you.'

He rolled me onto my back and pushed himself up inside me.

With his hand at my clit and his dick deep inside me, he fucked me hard until we both came, my body convulsing.

I lay shaking, my body quivering from orgasm after orgasm.

We fell asleep in each other's arms.

I loved this man with every fibre of my being; our souls are now one.

Jim dropped me home the next morning so I could get ready for work.

I closed the door and leaned against the wall in the hallway. I couldn't believe how amazing he was and how well things were going.

Julia crept back into my mind, but I banished her as quickly as possible. At least for the time being, she was out. I wouldn't worry about her again until I needed to.

Saturday was here again and it had arrived with plenty of nerves. I pushed the thoughts down, but they were never far away, creeping back to the forefront of my mind I was so excited about what was to come but also a little anxious.

My mind had been taken off it for the most part of the week, while prepping for my school talk. I had closed the shop for a few hours after I was unable to find anyone to cover. I had agonised over the decision, but I couldn't let the kids down, and, hopefully, it would bring them and their parents into the shop.

It had gone really well. I was expecting the kids to be hard work, with pointless questions that I had no answers for, but I was pleasantly surprised. They were the perfect audience. They ooohed and ahhhed in all the right places and asked very good questions after listening intently to my over-rehearsed speech.

One little girl, sat right at the back, had seemed to ignore everything I had said, more interested in whatever she was drawing.

She wore a denim dungaree dress over a striped long-sleeve top and her pigtails were askew, looking like they may have started in equal places but a morning of running around had seen to that.

At the end of the talk, I was packing away my things and putting on my jacket when she appeared at the desk.

'My name is Amy, this is for you,' she muttered, shoving a piece of paper at me.

'Thank you,' I said, turning it over to look.

A colourful pencil drawing stared back at me.

'That's you in your book shop,' she said, pointing at a stick figure holding a book. 'I'm going to ask my mum to bring me to visit you here,' she said.

'I would like that very much,' I told her.

She smiled and shook my hand, then ran off to join the rest of her class.

I thanked the headmaster for inviting me; I'd had a truly enjoyable time and hoped I was of some help to the children.

But now it was Saturday and I had no idea what to expect. I had packed an outfit for the evening and one for the next day, along with my toothbrush, razor and a few other shower essentials.

I had locked up the shop an hour early and I got into my car having texted Jim to say I was on my way. I nervously tapped my steering wheel, opting for some music to calm me.

Jim opened the door and put a glass of wine in my hand, after kissing me on the cheek.

We went into the bedroom and drank our wine together as Jim slowly undressed me, kissing along my neck and collar bone.

'I'll leave you to your shower, miss,' he said, turning on the radio. 'Enjoy!'

I got into the huge shower and turned on the jets. Hot water soaked my skin. I closed my eyes and inhaled the steam, melting away all my nerves.

I took my time and made the most of all the space, carefully lathering up with luxurious shower gel.

As I stepped out of the shower, I noticed him in the open doorway.

'I have a surprise for you,' he said with a mischievous grin.

He led me into the bedroom where a set of black lace underwear, complete with stockings and suspenders belt, lay on the bed.

'Put these on for me.'

I obliged, amazed at how well they fitted. He took my hair bobble out, letting my hair down around my shoulders, laid me down on the bed and kissed me, then pulled the wrist cuffs from under the mattress and secured my hands.

He walked to the end of the bed and did the same with my ankles, restraining my feet at each corner.

I squirmed with excitement as he came over and gently placed a blindfold over my eyes.

There was silence; he left the room. A few moments later, I heard the door quietly closing.

I could sense that I wasn't alone.

A gentle finger slid lightly across my stomach. I jumped at the touch.

Then another across my chest, just grazing the top of my breasts.

Now hands were stroking my thighs; very soft, gentle hands, not like the hard-working hands I was accustomed to.

He had brought someone else to play.

Panic started to spread through me, who was it?

A light fragrant perfume filled my nose.

He had brought another woman.

I felt my breath quicken, but fear was quickly replaced by something else...

Excitement.

I had never felt a woman's touch in this way, but had always wondered what it would be like.

How had he known? It was a fantasy I had never shared.

She was closing in on me and I felt her full lips on mine. Her tongue was invading my mouth and she tasted of strawberries.

She moved away, leaving me wanting more.

I didn't have to wait long.

She was back, hands pulling my tits out of my bra and into her mouth, one at a time, licking and sucking my nipples, sending waves of pleasure cascading between my legs.

I inhaled sharply and felt myself swell in anticipation, bucking my hips towards her.

I could feel her hands all over me and was desperate to return the favour, but, pulling at my restraints, I realised I had no chance.

Placing feathery light kisses down my stomach, my excitement grew.

Her fingers were stroking my inner thighs and her tongue was following.

She gently and seductively ran her tongue up the sides of my lace thong; I felt like I would explode with anticipation.

She didn't keep me waiting, pulling my underwear to the side. She stopped for a moment, affording me the time to realise I was on full display for her. The thought of her looking at me turned me on immensely.

I felt her skin against mine, letting me know she was wearing only underwear, or less.

I always thought that a woman would know exactly how a woman wanted to be touched and licked. I wasn't wrong; expertly she flicked her tongue over my clit and a deep moan escaped my lips.

I felt her hair brush against my leg as she licked and sucked at every part.

I rubbed against her face, desperate for more.

I was cumming in her mouth as she removed the blindfold.

I attempted to regain focus after being in the dark and post orgasm to see who my new friend was.

She wasn't blonde as I had imagined, but had long dark hair and was beautiful, dressed in underwear that mirrored mine, except red.

As I looked at her for the first time, I thought I should feel embarrassed, but didn't.

My gaze was drawn away from her to where Jim stood with his cock in his hand.

He was looking very pleased with himself as he walked over to uncuff my wrists, bare chested with his dick protruding from his fly.

Jim kissed me slowly and she released my feet.

He took a step back and watched as she climbed on top of me on all fours.

Hesitant at first, I reached up and touched her face.

She kissed me, this time tasting of me.

I stroked down her neck until I reached her pert breasts.

I ran my thumbs over her erect nipples and slowly rolled her bra down as the straps fell down her arms.

Her breasts felt good in my hands, heavy and full, but better in my mouth.

Her breathing quickened as I sucked each in turn.

Travelling down to her pants, I slipped my hand inside, parting her lips and drawing light circles on her clit.

Slowly I inserted one finger, then another and felt her clench around me as I found her swollen G-spot.

She humped and bucked her clit into my palm as I finger fucked her until she came into my hand.

It was time to taste her. I was nervous but also intrigued.

I lay her down on the bed and removed the red lace that

separated us.

Bending her knees, I spread her legs and looked at her neat little slit. Almost completely void of any hair, she had a little triangle doubling as an arrow pointing to the treasure.

As I moved my face closer, the smell of perfume on her skin mixed with the sweet scent of her pussy was a heady combination.

I started slowly, licking her slit from the bottom to the top in one motion, she bucked and inhaled sharply. She tasted so good, salty and warm.

I glanced at him, stood next to the bed, his hand wrapped tightly around his cock, slowly moving his fist up and down while licking his lips. He looked glorious watching us.
Every muscle in his arms and chest more beautiful than the last. My perfect man!

Feeling a little more daring this time, I put my tongue just inside her lips and licked all around, teasing and enjoying the taste.

I loitered around the opening to her tight little pussy and gently penetrated her.

She grabbed my head, pushing my tongue deep inside her. Out of the corner of my eye, I saw his hand getting quicker and quicker.

I loved knowing he was watching and wanking over us. She was writhing around the bed, panting and fucking my face.

She moaned as she came, freezing for a moment. She practically jumped up and pounced on me scissoring our legs and rubbing her clit against mine.

The sudden intense pleasure made me gasp.

He walked over and lifted my face to look at him, then rubbed his cock on my lip.

I greedily took him in my mouth and sucked him as if my life depended on it. Trying my hardest to concentrate, although the woman between my legs made that difficult. We furiously rubbed against each other, cumming together quickly.

He climbed up onto the bed, the muscles in his thighs flexing deliciously.

He looked at her, splayed naked on our bed, then at me. His eyes sparkled when I met his gaze.

He positioned her on her back with her feet at our pillows and helped me onto all fours into a 69.

I leaned over and buried my face back in her crotch, still slick with both our cum; she gasped and started sucking on my clit.

This time he knelt behind me and pushed his cock inside me, I had never felt so much pleasure.

I stopped eating her to be a little selfish.

A beautiful, busty brunette was sucking, licking and grinding her face on my clit while a gorgeous god of a man was filling me entirely with his rock-solid length. Pumping me hard and fast.

Feeling a little guilty, I put my fingers inside her pretty little cunt and the three of us came together. Violently. Shaking, shuddering and screaming.

I lay back on the bed, panting. I watched her go into the bathroom then re-emerge fully dressed a few minutes later.

Jim, wrapped in his robe, walked out of the room with her and I heard soft talking then the front door open and close again.

Jim came back in the room and sat next to me on the bed, stroking my hair.

He looked a little unsure. 'You OK?'

'Um, yeah, I think,' I replied, a little unsure myself.

Jim lay next to me on the bed and pulled me into his arms, holding me silently for what felt like hours.

I must have drifted off to sleep because I woke about an hour later. Jim was still next to me, propped up on one arm watching me sleep.

'How are you feeling now? Did I go too far?' He looked very worried.

I assessed the situation before answering. It was definitely different from anything I had ever experienced, but I most certainly enjoyed it. Surely that was clear to see. If I hadn't, I would have stopped her as soon as I realised.

Jim was staring intently at me, desperate for me to take away his agony and give him an answer.

'How did you know I would enjoy another woman?' were the only words to come out when I opened my mouth.

I saw him exhale with relief. 'Honestly? I didn't. My gut told me it was something you would enjoy. After that I just prayed I was right. If I had been wrong, it would have been a catastrophe.'

'You were right. I didn't know how much I would enjoy it. But who was she? Where do you find someone like that?'

'I have a friend,' he began. 'Gerry, he owns a club...a very particular club. I told him my plan and asked if there would be anyone he knew that could help out. He said he knew plenty and sent me some pictures. I decided on Verity, though I don't think that's her actual name.'

I thought about her name and decided that it suited her.

Real or not.

'Oh?' I said 'What kind of stuff happens at this club?'

'Well, it's kind of a fantasy club. From what he tells me, there is a variety of things that go on.'

'Like what?' my eyes widened.

'Um, bondage, dom/sub and uh...public displays.'

'So is that where you're planning our next date?' I said, giving him a playful dig in the ribs.

'Saskia,' he said looking into my eyes, 'I was going to wait a while before suggesting anything further. However, we can move at whatever speed you would like.'

'Well, I will definitely think about it.' I grinned at him.

The sparkle appeared in his eyes instantly.

'He has been asking me to visit ever since it opened, but I haven't got around to it – or maybe didn't fancy it alone.'

I imagined Jim by himself, coming back to this huge, empty apartment alone and felt a little sad. But now he was mine and I was his. I was ready to experience everything with this man.

He pushed me back onto the bed with one arm. 'You got some balls on you, girl,' he said, spreading my legs. 'I have to say, though, I felt like I was missing out on all the action. I could practically taste you watching her mouth on you.' He moved his face downwards and breathed in deeply. Slowly at first, he flicked his tongue around, then sped it up, darting over my clit and then inside me.

'Fuck, you taste so good,' he growled, alternating between nibbling my thigh and plunging his tongue back inside me.

I'm not sure how I had the energy but soon I was cumming again. Then he flipped me onto my stomach and pushed himself up inside me. I could feel his hot breath on the back of my neck as he thrust until he was empty again.

I was suddenly aware of how hungry I was, my stomach growling in agreement.

Jim smiled and lifted me up off the bed, carrying me into the bathroom. I wasn't exactly huge, but he did it with ease, like a child carrying a doll.

He placed me on the cold tiles, wrapped me in a fluffy towel and told me to come down when I was ready.

I cleaned myself up, then dressed, practically running in response to the smell of his cooking.

He was stood at the worktop, seasoning pork chops when I walked in.

I stood and watched him for a moment. He looked as delicious as the food smelled. His jeans hung low around his waist and his black t shirt clung to every muscle.

'Can I help?' I offered.

'You just take a seat, beautiful.' He arranged some salad on the plate with new potatoes, then added the pork.

After another delicious meal, I sat back feeling exhausted. It felt like it must be very late, but the clock proved me wrong, showing it was just gone 8.30 p.m.

Jim cleared away the plates and returned to the table with fresh fruit and some ice cream, which was a real treat.

He finished his dessert, then wandered back into his bedroom. I followed him and found him in the en suite, running a bath. Lavender wafted around the bathroom and there were candles on the windowsill.

It was a giant freestanding bath with a roll top. I certainly wasn't going to refuse. A bath was exactly what I needed.

He undressed me and helped me in, stripping and getting in behind me. He pulled my hair up on top of my head and secured it with a bobble, then kissed my neck and shoulders. I lay back onto his chest and we stayed that way, in silence. Breathing in the beautiful fragrance, unable to make out much around the bathroom with the mixture of steam and candlelight.

I sat forward to stop myself drifting off and he squeezed a soapy sponge onto my shoulders and back, then lathered the bubbles all over my skin, reaching under my arms and massaging my breasts.

When he was done, he rinsed me off with the big brass shower head that had been sitting on top of the posh taps. One hand reached down to my stomach, then moved down to tease my clit. As my body reacted to his touch, he pulled the shower head under the water and focused the jets between my legs. I bucked at the new pleasure and water sloshed over the edges of the bath onto the white tiles.

He didn't seem to notice, holding the shower in place with one hand and putting the other to good use, rolling my nipple between his finger and thumb.

I came silently this time, questioning how many more times I could in one day.

Seemingly happy that I was done, he got out of the bath and threw a towel onto the spilled water. Still naked and dripping wet, he lifted me out, wrapped me in a robe and placed me on the bed.

I watched as he walked around the room, towel drying his hair but letting his body air dry. It was a pleasure to watch him. I don't think had ever seen a more beautiful man. I had always preferred a man in underwear as I had never found a dick that pretty to look at. As I lay there watching him, I realised that I had just been looking at the wrong ones. He was perfect and I knew this tease was just for my pleasure.

He placed one of his t-shirts on the bed next to me and I thanked him and stood up to remove my robe. His turn to watch, and he did with a smile as I dried off and slipped the tee over my head.

Fortunately, he could see my exhaustion and pulled me close to him, passing the remote to me so I could pick a film.

He traced his fingers over my arm. 'I am so in love with you, Saskia. Every part of you.'

'I'm very happy to report that I'm feeling the same, Mr Edwards.'

Chapter 12

I woke Sunday morning to find Jim snoring lightly beside me. I realised that I had never seen him sleep before as he was always up first. I watched his chest rise and fall and his eyelashes flutter slightly. He must have felt my eyes on him, as he woke quickly.

He glanced across to his bedside table and laughed.

'What's so funny?'

'I just can't remember the last time I slept this late! We must have used a lot of energy last night.'

I sat up and looked over him. It was gone 11 a.m.! 'Jeez, it's almost lunchtime!' I said, feeling guilty about sleeping so late.

'Get dressed then, you,' he teased, clearly noticing my surprise at the time.

'I need food, and I would love it if you would join me.'

We dressed and left the apartment, walking round the corner to the little pub. 'They serve the best Sunday dinner around,' Jim said, as his stomach growled at the thought.

'Hi, Jim,' the barmaid said as we walked through the doors of his local. She waved us to a table towards the corner of the room.

It was quite a small pub, very busy. It smelled of beer and peanuts and wasn't light and airy, but friendly all the same.

We sat at a table for two with just enough room for our

drinks next to our plates which were soon piled high with sliced beef, roasties and veg, swimming in thick, luscious gravy.

'I'm ready,' I announced.

Jim looked up with a forkful of beef.

'Ready?'

'Yes,' I said, biting my bottom lip. 'I'm ready to go to this club.'

'Oh,' he said, putting his fork back onto his plate. 'Oh, OK.' His lips turned up into a smile.

'When would you like to go?'

'This weekend?' I said casually.

'This weekend it is,' he said. 'I'll give Gerry a call, let him know to expect us.'

After what really was the best Sunday dinner I'd had – except my mum's, of course – we left the pub and went back to Jim's. I packed my things and got in my little car to go home, needing rest and respite before work again tomorrow.

Our date at Gerry's club was getting closer and the normal nerves had surfaced. The shop had started to pick up with the holidaymakers in town and my days were disappearing at lightning speed.

Jim had called into the shop Wednesday morning with a white box, tied with a red ribbon, asking me to wear what was inside.

He had warned me that there was a dress code and it might make me uncomfortable, so to open it before Saturday and let him know if I wanted something else.

I sat on my bed Wednesday evening and gingerly opened the box. I removed the pink tissue paper and immediately grinned at the beautiful silver peep-toe heels staring back at me. I pulled them out and saw a mass of black silk beneath them. I lifted it out and was pleasantly surprised by how much it would actually cover, expecting a lot worse. Fresh out of the shower, I undid my robe and slipped it on with the shoes.

He had done it again. It all fitted perfectly and was so flattering, hugging what little curves I had. It had a sweetheart top, showing cleavage but still leaving a little to the imagination. It cinched in at the waist with lace panels on each side down to a skater-type skirt that ended just below my arse cheeks. It must have cost a small fortune.

I studied myself in the mirror, noticing my body shape had changed; pulled in at the waist slightly and my stomach was more toned. Must be all the sex; they do say it's the best form of exercise.

I put my arms above my head and turned slightly, revealing my bare ass. Well I better remember to keep my arms down Saturday night, I laughed to myself. I noticed more silk protruding from the pink tissue on the box and pulled out a G-string. I didn't have to look long to see it wasn't like any G-string I owned; instead of the little bit of cotton to cover any modesty, there was a string of pearls, I put it on, the smooth beads sitting just inside my lips.

I stared at my reflection, wondering whether I was brave enough to leave the house like this, let alone go into a club. One minute I was shaking my head, telling myself I was ridiculous for even contemplating the idea, the next my head was telling me fuck it, just do it.

I looked in the mirror again and thought how hard I had worked to get and maintain the figure looking back at me and decided that if I didn't go and do it wearing this, it would be something I would regret.

I typed a message out to Jim and hit Send.

Thank you for my new outfit. Let's hope it's not too breezy Saturday evening. X

Instantly my phone informed me Jim was typing.

So you will wear it? X

As long as I can wear a coat to get there X

Of course. I'll pick you up at 7 then? X

Having confirmed with Jim, I took a picture of myself in my new outfit, enjoying the feel of the silk and pearls before taking it off and hanging it up in the wardrobe.

I heard the front door close and Beth shout up.

I pulled on my lounge pants and a vest top and went down to meet her, calling hello on the way.

We sat at the kitchen table and Beth made us both a cup of tea. Matt was visiting his parents and wouldn't be back until the weekend.

'So, do you have any plans this weekend?' she asked, mug in hand.

'Jim and I are off out, I'm not sure where yet though,' I said, fighting my conscience a little. I hated lying to my best friend, but I didn't want to share this.

'Well, I can't wait to hear all about it,' she squealed. 'Ben and I are having a night in on the sofa, we've been out too much lately and are ready for a takeaway and a bottle of wine.'

'Ah, did I miss the big day?' I teased. 'Can't believe you didn't ask me to be bridesmaid!'

'Yes, I know!' she said, laughing, 'The party girl doesn't want to party. I just feel really settled and comfortable.' Adoration shone from her eyes as she spoke about Ben.

'I'm so happy for you,' I said, giving her a squeeze.

I got home just after five, I went up and showered. Meticulously shaving away as much hair as possible, ready for goodness knows what tonight.

I slathered my skin in moisturiser and paced the floorboards while it dried. Was I ready for this? I was feeling so nervous I was actually shaking. My phone started buzzing. I looked down to see Jim's picture on my screen. It was as if he just knew.

'Hi, Saskia, are you OK?' he asked softly.

'Um, I think so,' I lied.

Clearly seeing straight through me, he continued, 'We don't have to go. If you have changed your mind, that's fine. Honestly.'

I took a deep breath, trying to steady my wavering voice 'No, I want to go. I'm just soooooo nervous.'

'That's only natural. Shall I come over for six instead and bring some wine?'

'I would love nothing more.'

True to his word, Jim arrived at the front door just before six with a bottle of wine.

He was wearing a pair of ripped jeans and, to my delight, when he removed his jacket there was nothing but his tight abs underneath. He blushed a little.

'Dress code for men too.'

We sat in my bedroom with a glass each, gradually refilling until there was no more. Jim made me feel so safe. I'm sure the wine played its part, but just his presence calmed my nerves.

Feeling a lot braver, I took my outfit and shoes into the bathroom and put them on. A flutter of nerves and excitement washed over me. I slowly walked back into my room where Jim was waiting for me. He looked me up and down.

'Wow, Saskia, I'm not sure I want you to leave the house,' he said, laughing. 'You look amazing! How do you feel?'

'The wine helped, and you too. I think I'm ready. Let's do this!'

Jim helped me into my long tan coat and I instantly felt covered up enough to leave – although it probably looked a little suspect in the warm weather.

A taxi pulled up outside and I locked up as Jim opened the car door.

The club was around a half an hour drive away, so we settled in on the back seat, Jim placing his hand over mine soothingly.

The car slowed to a stop and I looked out of the window to see what looked like a large manor house. There was no sign that it was anything other than that. A gated driveway led up to the house, with perfectly cut grass around it and large planters either side of the doorway.

Jim paid the driver and we both got out, staring up at the house as it loomed down on us.

He linked his arm through mine and we walked up to the door. There was an old-fashioned doorbell that you had to pull to announce your arrival. Jim pulled it and we took a step back.

The door started to open and there was a man standing on the other side with a clipboard. He was buff and a little mean-looking, but politely asked for our names. Quickly finding us on his list, he asked us to wait just inside and called into his radio. We were stood in a wide entrance hall. It was light and airy and had an upmarket feel to it. Large, brightly coloured abstract paintings donned the walls, making it look as though an interior decorator had landed a dream job here.

I was surprised to see how modern everything was inside. The bright, spacious entrance hall was decorated with flowers and modern art and there was a large white double door in the middle of the wall.

A few moments later, a sandy-haired man appeared. He was tall and lean, yet muscular at the same time. He sported black trousers and a loose white shirt, undone and tucked into his waistband, showing his six-pack beneath it.

'Jim Edwards!' he exclaimed. 'How long has it taken to get you here?'

'Gerry,' Jim said, shaking his hand. 'It has been too long, and for that I apologise.'

Jim squeezed my hand. 'This is Saskia.'

'What a pleasure to meet you, Saskia,' Gerry said, shaking my hand warmly.

'You are both very welcome and, as my personal guests, please help yourselves to whatever you would like from the bar. It's on me tonight.'

I thanked him feeling very self-conscious, knowing that this man I'd just met knew all about my girl action a couple of weeks ago, possibly in full detail.

As Gerry led us further in, I could hear soft music coming from inside.

Gerry opened the doors and I strained to see inside. It was a lot darker in there, which was a blessing as Gerry was asking to take our coats. Jim handed over his, but I hesitated and Jim felt my unease. I didn't want to fall at the first hurdle so undid my coat and took it off, passing it to Gerry. He glanced at me, but said nothing as he took it.

'Please, enjoy yourselves and let me know if you need

anything.' he said, smiling.

Jim led me through the door and my eyes began to adjust to the dimly lit room. It was quite a large room.

There was a long bar running most of the way down the wall to my right and lots of sofas dotted around, some with tables next to them.

Not surprisingly, I didn't feel incorrectly dressed for the occasion. There were half-naked people everywhere I looked, some making me feel I was covering up too much.

We followed Gerry to the bar and he told the barman we were his guests tonight and left us to it.

The barman serving us smiled and introduced himself as Harry. He had dark hair and was dressed in a pair of black trousers that hugged his bum tightly. Like all the other men in the club – except Gerry – he was topless. I figured that Gerry wanted to stand out as the owner of the club and therefore wore his shirt like some sort of statement.

Jim ordered some shots of tequila and a bottle of Corona each and found a sofa that wasn't too central so we could settle in.

He lined up two shots each and raised one of the little glasses. I picked up mine and giggled; we clinked and drank up, downing the second straight after.

'Right,' he said. 'Hopefully that will calm the nerves.'

I smiled at him and we both sat there, taking in our surroundings.

A few sofas away from us, a couple caught my eye. A woman who looked to be in her forties, dressed in a pale-pink silk baby doll, was sat with her back to a man around the same age, in between his legs. He was kissing her neck and fondling her breasts, one of which was on full display. As I watched, I noticed his other hand moving up her thigh and rubbing between her legs.

Suddenly realising I was staring, I quickly averted my eyes only to find Jim had been watching me the whole time. I blushed and avoided eye contact.

'Hey, don't be embarrassed,' he said sweetly. 'It's why we're here, right?'

I nodded, searching for somewhere else to look but everywhere seemed to contain a similar sight.

'I wonder what's down there,' I said, doing my best to change the subject and gesturing towards the back of the room where it seemed to taper off to another corridor.

'We can finish our drinks and go investigate if you like?' he said, picking up his beer bottle.

I nodded again, trying my best to feel brave about the whole situation.

We sat and talked while drinking and Jim told me how he knew Gerry. They had met in college and he was always a lady's man, swearing then that he would somehow make a career from his love of women.

As we both finished our drinks, I felt the alcohol take hold and my courage return.

'Come on then, let's go have a look, shall we?' I said, smiling at Jim and standing up. He didn't need any more encouragement as he stood up beside me.

We walked around a bit, taking in the view of couples and groups of people, very obviously enjoying their night. But something was pulling me to the back of the room. I needed to know what was down there. As we got closer, Gerry appeared by my side, and, as if reading my mind, said, 'There are booths down there. Come on, I'll show you.'

We followed him back as he continued, 'Booths with beds, tables, chairs, desks and basically anything you can "play" on. They're all open to "viewing". There are a few available if you're feeling brave, or some occupied if you want to take it a bit slower.'

I opened my mouth to speak, but my breath caught in my throat so I followed silently.

The first booth contained an examination table and a light on a stand with wheels, but was empty of people.

The next room was definitely putting on a show as there were a couple of people watching outside and the gasps of pleasure were hard to miss.

I wasn't sure I was ready to see what was inside, but there was no going back now.

As we got closer I could see the light pouring out from the room, illuminating the onlookers. There was unalloyed pleasure on their faces as they watched; clearly they were enjoying what I couldn't yet see. There were two men watching; one rubbing at his crotch and the other with his arms around a woman stood in front of him. They didn't seem to notice us, too engaged in the show.

Inside the booth, a woman was sat facing her audience on a high-backed stool, legs splayed and the stilettos of her shoes hooked onto the stool's foot bar. Her head was thrown back in pleasure as she groaned. She had a corset on, accentuating her voluptuous figure. Her tits were bouncing around above the top of the corset, nipples erect. She had fishnet stockings on and there was a man kneeling in front of her. He was buff as hell and wearing tight black Y-fronts. He was holding her legs apart and greedily licking and sucking at her pussy.

I instantly felt a pull between my legs as I watched. Completely forgetting where I was, I jumped as Jim touched my shoulder and brought me back to the ground again.

I looked around, but Gerry had left us. Jim didn't say a word, just stood behind me with his hand on my shoulder.

The woman cried out as the man teamed his tongue with his fingers inside her, bringing her to orgasm right there while we all watched.

He got up, giving the spectators a full view of her slit, still wet from his work. I looked at her face for the first time; she was staring out into the crowd that was now forming, truly loving the attention.

He stood her up and took her place on the stool, removing his pants to reveal his huge cock. She turned to face him and lifted the baby doll around her waist before straddling him and lowering herself onto him, gasping as she took his length.

As I continued to watch, my crotch throbbing with the need to be touched, Jim kissed the back of my neck and my temperature sky-rocketed. I grabbed his hand and thrust it inside the cup of my top; as his fingers found my nipple, my stomach tightened.

The woman was now bouncing up and down on the man's cock, using the foot bars to support herself. They were both moaning loudly until they reached their climax, then she stood up over him, letting his cum pour out of her.

The group started to disperse and Jim led me back to the main room. He ordered us another beer and sat us both down on the nearest sofa. 'Did you enjoy that?' he asked, already knowing the answer.

'Very much so,' I said, smiling as I sipped my beer. I wanted to be back in the corridor, finding more to watch. Jim grabbed my face, kissing me deeply. His hand went inside my top, pulling my breast out and lowering his mouth to my nipple. I looked around but no one was watching. I wasn't sure if I felt relieved or disappointed. He trailed his hand down my stomach and lightly ran his fingers down the line of pearls. The feeling was exquisite and I was desperate for more. I opened my legs for him, secretly hoping someone was watching, and he slowly rubbed his thumb over the little beads, repeatedly from the top to as far down as he could get. He hadn't yet touched me, but I was so close to cumming for him.

He clearly read the signs, but, instead of helping me to my finish, he stopped and picked up his beer. Feeling flustered, I sat up and did the same. We didn't speak as we finished our drinks and with unspoken agreement we got up and went back towards the corridor.

This time it was two blonde girls and a Spanish-looking man. They were all naked, lying on a big bed together. He had one girl bent over and was fucking her from behind while she had her head burrowed deep between the other blonde's thighs, eating hungrily.

I felt like I was going to explode; the need to be touched was so intense that I couldn't help but move my own hand down.

Jim grabbed my hand and tapped the back gently, shaking his head at me. Why was he torturing me like this?

He stood close behind me, holding my hands behind my back. Finding his bulging cock took my mind off my own pleasure as I unzipped his jeans and teased him with my fingers. He held me in place, enjoying my hands until the threesome was over. My desire was now at a height I never knew it could reach.

'You want to find an empty booth?' he asked, his voice gruff with yearning and his eyes full of the sparkle I loved.

'Yes,' I said, feeling more certain than ever. 'I really do.'

He led me down the corridor, passing a few occupied booths until we reached one with no bed or desk. Just a backless bar stool and straps coming from a bar close to the ceiling. He looked at me with excitement and I knew this was it. This was going to be my first public appearance.

I wondered if anyone would watch, but was too horny to worry about it.

We went in and he stood me up against the wall. He fixed my hands above my head with the straps and my feet to a spreader bar on the floor. With my 'keep your arms down' rule well and truly broken, my pearl crotchless thong was most definitely no longer covered.

He stood back and looked at me a while, rubbing the front of his jeans making his bulge grow. I was watching him so intently that I hadn't noticed the people outside. There were at least three people stood watching us.

Excitement washed over me and I could practically feel myself dripping, I was so wet with excitement.

He started by removing my tits, one by one from their sweetheart top, filling his hands with them, then his mouth.

Already weak with desperation, I pulled at my restraints.

He ran both hands down my sides over the lace panels and to my hips, then around to cup my arse.

Then, again with just one finger, he gently touched every pearl on the string, carefully pushing one at a time into my clit. As if highlighting this to my voyeurs, he repeated it once more. I looked up to see there were another five or six people watching and one of them was Gerry.

Before I could start to feel embarrassed, Jim was on the floor in front of me, licking up my thighs, getting closer and closer to where I needed him to be. I tried to move into his mouth but he moved backwards, pulling the string of pearls from the back.

I unwillingly let out a low moan as the beads pulled tightly against my clit. He pushed two fingers inside me, making me quiver, then ran his tongue all the way up the string, giving me the opportunity to thrust into his open mouth. Finally giving in to me, he licked and sucked around the pearls, then pulled the pants down past my knees, getting straight back in there to eat up all he could. The feeling was so intense I had forgotten the people watching as I came hard into his mouth, his fingers pounding at my G-spot.

When he was satisfied that I was done, he uncuffed me, pulled my thong off my heels and led me to the stool, facing me away from the crowd now forming. The stool was quite high and the top reached my waist. Looking deeply into my eyes he asked quietly, 'Are you OK, Saskia?'

'More than OK,' I replied.

He smiled.

'I love you, beautiful,' he said as he tucked a stray hair behind my ear.

'I love you too,' I said, as he bent me over the stool. Knowing there were now over ten people stood just feet away from my display made my heart pound. I saw his jeans and boxers drop to the floor where he kicked them off and imagined how he looked, stood there naked and beautiful for everyone to see. I enjoyed the fact they could look, but only I could touch.

His feet disappeared from my view and I felt him turn the stool side on. He was behind me now, opening me up as he slid his length inside me. I welcomed him in; the feeling of him filling me was magnificent.

As he pounded away, I lifted my head slightly to see if my crowd were enjoying the show. To my delight, there wasn't one person just stood there, every one of them was engaged in some form of masturbation as they watched. Although Gerry was nowhere to be seen.

Jim had found that sweet spot, as he always did, and hit it while his fingers found my clit. He had never been loud in bed but I could hear him now, growling out my name and cumming into me as I lost all control and squeezed him tightly as I reached climax.

Before I could think, I was being stood up and wrapped in a gown and led out of the room. But it wasn't Jim that had covered me up, it was Gerry.

'Well, angel. You sure that's your first time?' he asked. 'You're a natural. First-timers usually struggle to climax for their audience, but not you.'

His smile turned my stomach.

Jim was by my side again and Gerry patted him on the back. 'Nice show, mate. You should have joined us years ago.' Gerry winked at me and turned to walk away, but not before I noticed the bulge in his jeans.

I suddenly felt exhausted and Jim guided me back to the bar and asked for some water. We sat and drank quickly as Jim looked at me, concerned.

'How are you feeling, Saskia?'

'Very tired,' I admitted.

'Shall I call a taxi?'

'Yes, I think I'm ready to go home. If that's OK with you?'

'Of course it is. It's nearly midnight anyway, and we have had quite a night.'

Jim practically lifted me into the taxi and I rested my head on his shoulder. By the time we'd pulled up outside his apartment, I had drifted off to sleep. He paid the driver and helped me in through the door.

'Go on into bed, beautiful,' he said, kindly.

I peeled myself out of my lingerie and got in the shower, pulling my hair into a bun on the top of my head.

Feeling fresher, I pulled on an oversized shirt Jim had left out for me and crawled into his bed.

Jim joined me a few minutes later, carrying a tray with cheese and crackers and two mugs of tea.

He put the tray down and got in beside me.

We ate silently, and, once I had finished the last of my tea, I finally felt my energy coming back.

'Do you want to talk about it?'

I laughed inside, thinking: *I must have hit the jackpot with this one*. How many men asked their women if they wanted to talk?

'Thank you for my food and tea. I feel so much better,' I told him.

'And don't look so worried.' I laughed softly, stroking the distressed look from his face. 'I have never done anything like that in my life, but, I have to say, I thoroughly enjoyed every minute. And I don't even feel embarrassed to admit it.'

'I'm so glad, Saskia,' he said, breathing a sigh of relief. 'I really was worried that it had upset you. I really enjoyed it too. Seeing all those people practically salivating over you was such a turn-on.'

Jim had a quick shower, then suggested a film. In true Saskia style, I was asleep within twenty minutes, before the alcohol could wear off completely.

Chapter 13

Beth was in that Sunday.

'What are you up to today, Sass?' she asked, buttering two pieces of toast, putting them onto a plate and offering them to me.

'Absolutely nothing,' I declared happily, taking a slice of toast and biting into it.

'You fancy taking a picnic to the park to enjoy the sun and catch up?'

'Awesome idea,' I told her through a mouthful. 'I'll make some sandwiches.'

'Great, I'm just about to make some of those little Victoria Sponges, we can take those too,' she said, getting up and turning the oven on to heat up.

Before long, we were sat soaking up the sun eating mini sandwiches and cakes.

I had found a bottle of Prosecco in the fridge which we sipped on from plastic champagne flutes and we even had strawberries to nibble on. Summer was in the air; I could smell freshly cut grass and barbecues and there were sounds of laughter from a group of children kicking a ball around.

Happy shrieks could be heard over a radio pumping out Jazzy Jeff and The Fresh Prince. The epitome of summer.

'So,' Beth said, sitting cross-legged on our tartan picnic blanket, having caught up on everything except the previous night. 'Where did he take you?'

My face flushed instantly as I recalled the events of the previous night.

Memories of being tied up in the booth and cumming for my audience flooded back, sending quivers down to my core.

I definitely didn't want to share this with Beth. I wasn't sure if I was worried about what she would think of me, or if it just wasn't something I wanted to share, but out came more lies.

'Oh, you know, pub dinner then Netflix and chill.'

We sat until it started to get a little cooler, then went back home; Beth leaving to spend the rest of the afternoon with Ben.

For the remainder of my Sunday I cleaned the house and settled down to eat my dinner.

I was sat reading when I heard the door open and Matt announced himself.

He looked tired and fed up.

'Hey, how are you doing?' I asked sympathetically.

'Ah, not great, Sass. I'm trying so hard to hate her, but I just miss her.'

I got up and walked over to him, sitting on the back of the sofa.

'Have you heard from her at all?'

'She's called and messaged so many times. I've just ignored them though. I can't be with someone who would hide something like that. I don't understand what she thought would happen. Maybe she never intended for me to find out.'

He leaned over and rested his forehead on my shoulder.

I patted the back of his head. 'I know what you need, my

boy,' I announced, getting up and walking into the kitchen.

I rummaged around in the freezer drawers and found the tub of ice cream I had been keeping for an emergency just like this. I grabbed two spoons and went back into the front room.

'Ben and Jerry are the best people to know at times like this. Dig in.' I smiled and handed him the tub and a spoon.

He took the ice cream and did just that, ripping the lid off and tossing it on the table. 'You got anything to take my mind off the bitch?' he asked. 'Any gossip?'

I laughed. 'Well, as it happens, I do. Although I'm not sure how you feel about hearing it,' I said. 'It may be a little too much info for you.' I already felt I'd said too much.

He looked worried. 'Oh god. What have you done?'

I had known this man most of my life and had always told him everything, even cringey sex stuff. I confided in him more than Beth as he always had a very impartial view. I put this down to the fact he was a man. He never just told me what he thought I wanted to hear. I had always felt like I could trust him. It would be nice to have someone else to confide in about this.

I took a deep breath and gave him a rundown on everything that had happened since the charity do.

When I had finished, I looked up at him, hoping he wasn't disgusted with me.

'Well, I have to say, Sass, I never thought you would be into anything like that,' he said with a grin on his face.

'You're not revolted by me?'

Matt laughed 'Not at all, Sass. I just wish I had known your thoughts on it all before!'

'Why do you say that?' I asked, confused.

He passed me the ice cream tub, sat back in the chair,

stretched and laughed again, a little nervously.

'Ah, Sass, I have so much to tell you.'

I looked at him, waiting for the big revelation.

'Um, OK, so go for it, the suspense is killing me!'

'You remember Dan and Xavier from school?' he started.

I nodded, fully engrossed.

'Well we were all having some beers in the bar one evening, we were only about eighteen. Dan tells me that some cougar is eyeing me up so I look over to see this woman. She was quite a bit older but she was so hot. Like a glamour model.

She raised her glass to me and smiled. I was going to leave it at that but the boys kept on at me to go over. You know, teenage boy hormones raging and all.'

'So you went over?'

'Yes. She told me her name was Maddison and that she was looking for some company.'

'What did you say?' I demanded, desperate to hear more.

'Well, as I said, teenage boy hormones raging...and she was hot! I told her I would keep her company.'

'And???'

'And we had a few drinks and she started stroking my leg, then asked me how old I was. She didn't flinch when I told her I was eighteen so I asked how old she was and she told me she was thirty-seven.'

He smiled as he remembered and continued, 'She asked if I wanted to go back to her place, and, clearly being led by my dick, I told her I did. She lived in this amazing, huge house and I started to panic a bit. I asked her who she lived with and she gave this deep, throaty laugh and told me she lived alone and that she wasn't married or involved with anyone.

We had some crazy, dirty sex. I mean, I hadn't had much experience at this point, but even looking back, it was pure filth.'

I was literally on the edge of my seat. 'So what happened next?'

'She called me a cab and paid the fare before I left. I felt like some kind of escort, but also didn't really care. A few days later, she called me and asked me if I wanted to hook up again. I went straight to her house and we had sex all evening, then she paid for my taxi home again. It happened a few times. Then she asked if I wanted to go to this club she belonged to. She said it was a little out there, but she thought I would enjoy it.'

I stared at him, wide-eyed. I was lost for words.

'By the sounds of where Jim took you, it was a very similar sort of deal. I was really nervous, but once I was in there, I couldn't believe my eyes. It was like all my birthdays had come at once. Just imagine an eighteen-year-old boy walking through a club filled with people fucking openly and wanting to be watched. It was like a dream.

'We took it slow to start, just watching others, but soon we were performing and sharing each other around. I more than doubled my magic number within my first few visits.'

Hardly able to believe what I was hearing, I asked him, 'What happened to her, then?'

'Her mum got sick and she moved away to care for her. I never heard from her again. But by that time, I was a fully-fledged member of the club and having far too much fun to stop. So I kept going and playing my part, sleeping with two or three girls a night. I even got my picture on the wall as Fuck of the Month, six months running.'

He smiled proudly and leaned back on the sofa.

I was flabbergasted. 'But you didn't tell me because you thought I wouldn't approve?'

'Yeah, you were kinda straightlaced back then when it came to sex, pretty vanilla, you know?' He punched my arm gently. 'Clearly things have changed though, hey, Sass.'

I looked down, suddenly feeling embarrassed again.

'So do you still attend such clubs?'

'Nah, I stopped a good few years ago. I wanted something real, you know? And I really thought I had found that in Stacey.' He hung his head, looking like a kid who had just lost his pet fish.

I put an arm around him.

'It will get better,' I promised.

'Yeah, I know. Just a shit journey,' he said, taking the ice cream tub from me and digging his spoon in again.

After quite the catch-up with Matt, we said goodnight and went into our rooms.

I lay in bed thinking about the weekend I'd had. Jim had messaged to say goodnight and that he was really glad the weekend went well. I thought again about the club and the enormity of what we had done and tried to work through my feelings about it all.

I kept coming to the same conclusion; I wanted to go back again. I felt there was so much more to experience.

I thought again about Jim and how I would feel with his involvement and decided that I was comfortable enough that it was something I would like to experiment with. I responded to Jim telling him that I loved him and was maybe ready to take it up a notch. He responded to say that he loved me too and was ready for whatever I wanted.

I closed the shop door behind me Monday morning and breathed in that beautiful book smell. I was ready for whatever the week threw at me. It was a warm day so I had decided on my white linen trousers and a pale-pink vest top. Feeling relieved I had dressed lightly, I wedged the shop door open, allowing a breeze to flow through.

I picked up the post, tied my hair up into a ponytail, and did my usual clean around. Once the shelves were dust free and I'd made a list of what stock I needed, I made myself a coffee and sat down to open the mail. Mostly junk as usual, with a bill thrown in. But there was one envelope that took my interest. I opened it up and looked inside. It was a letter from a company I had previously worked with, inviting me to take part in their next book convention. I had done them a few times before and they had been lots of fun and pretty good for sales. This one was a little further away so would require a hotel overnight and some help. If I could get Beth or Matt to help out, I would go for it.

I sent them both a text asking if they were available for the weekend in a month's time and told them I would pay them.

Beth responded quickly saying that she and Ben were away with his family that weekend and she was really sorry she couldn't help. Matt replied just after her, saying, 'No plans, Sass, I'm all yours.'

I responded to them both and thanked Matt, saying I was looking forward to it.

I emailed the company to confirm my place and paid the deposit, then spent the rest of the day adding everything I thought I would need for the con to my order list and sent it off to my suppliers.

I found a cheap and cheerful hotel right near the venue and

booked two single rooms, then sent Matt the details.

Feeling very accomplished, I locked up the shop and went home, calling in at the supermarket on the way to grab some essentials.

When I got home, Matt was in his room. I called to him to say I was making vegetable lasagne for dinner and invited him to join me.

I wanted to do something nice for him for agreeing to help out with the con and, also, he was still feeling really down so thought I'd try and cheer him up.

Matt inhaled his food, as he always did.

When we had finished, he rocked back on two legs of his chair.

'So what happens at these conventions then?'

'It's basically like two days of a car boot sale, but with books,' I said, laughing.

'Except people are a little more reserved than a car boot sale,' I backtracked, remembering the trip to the local boot sale Beth and I had done a few years back.

We had got up super early to set up our pitch, but, by the time we had got there, the place was teeming with people and they were looking through the car windows for bargains before we had even parked up.

I shuddered at the memory. I would not be doing that again.

I went to bed thinking about Jim and what our next adventure would be like.

I closed my eyes and was back in the booth at the club with people stood watching.

I pulled down my covers and let the warm air travel over my naked body.

Slowly I ran through scenarios in my head; Jim tying me up again and letting other people into the booth.

I imagined how it would feel to have him watch as other men touched and tasted me.

My hands travelled down to my crotch to find I was very wet at these thoughts.

I slowly slipped my finger inside, while rubbing my clit with the palm of my hand.

I came quickly and silently, letting the aftershocks set off a second orgasm.

I fell into a deep sleep, dreaming about the possibilities.

Chapter 14

I woke up Tuesday morning in the middle of a hot and steamy dream, annoyed I hadn't got to enjoy the ending and in much need of my actual ending.

I decided that I had a spare five minutes before I had to get up, and fished around in the drawer under my bed, looking for my old faithful battery-operated friend. It couldn't replace the touch of my man, but was great for a much-needed quick release.

I rubbed the end of the vibrator on my clit and pressed the button, my orgasm started building instantly and within a few moments, I was cumming silently once more.

Now I was ready to start my day.

I met Jim after work, nervous about telling him my thoughts on sharing him. It was definitely getting easier to discuss my desires with him, but it still brought colour to my cheeks as he stared at me, intently listening and, so far, agreeing to whatever I wanted.

Just the thought of seeing him was enough to get my temperature rising. I didn't even have to close my eyes to conjure fantastic fuck flashbacks these days. In fact, I struggled keeping the thoughts out of my head enough to get on with my daily routine.

We had eaten another beautifully cooked meal and were lounging around on his sofa when he gave me the silence I needed to strike up my courage and conversation.

'So, I've been thinking a lot about Gerry's place,' I began while absentmindedly running my finger over the stitching on the cushions and into the holes where the buttons were fastened.

Jim gave me his full attention. 'Have you now?'

'Mmm hmm. And I think I would like to pay another visit,' I said, trying to sound nonchalant while suppressing my blush.

'OK, that's fine with me,' he said, running his fingers down my arm.

'I think maybe we could try some other stuff too... If that's OK with you of course,' I muttered, unable to conceal my reddening cheeks this time.

His eyes sparkled – would he be put out at my sudden yen for other people? Would he feel like he wasn't enough for me?

'What did you have in mind, Saskia?' he asked sweetly.

'Well, if you're not comfortable with it, it's completely fine; it was just a thought.' This was that time to stop talking again.

'Just say it, Sass, you should know by now that I'm pretty open-minded!' He laughed.

'OK, well, I was thinking about maybe involving some other people, you know, like maybe another couple.' I winced as I said it, instantly wishing I could take it back.

'Saskia,' he started, a serious look on his face. 'I love you, and only you. As long as you know that, I am happy to involve whoever you would like to.'

I exhaled and looked at him. 'I love you too. And only you. I also love how different our sex life is,' I admitted with a grin.

'Then that's settled. When do you want to go?'

I giggled. 'Any plans this weekend?'

We decided on Friday night and he went into the kitchen to make us a cup of tea. I followed him in and watched him filling the glass kettle and flicking it on, the blue glow emanating from it lighting up the corner of the worktop.

He reached up into the top cupboard to get our mugs down and his abs peeked out from under his t-shirt.

Unable to resist, I ran my hands up his chest while I stood behind him.

He turned to face me and leaned against the worktop. On my tiptoes, I reached up and kissed him, letting my hands wander up to his shoulders and remove his top.

The sight of him stood there in his jeans set my temperature rising. My hands now at his waist, I pulled his button and fly undone, then reached inside the warmth of his boxers to his semi-hard cock.

I pulled it out and got down onto my knees. The kettle was bubbling furiously as I licked my way up his shaft, feeling him harden fully.

I wanted him way more than I wanted tea right now so I closed my lips around his head and sucked him in deep. He groaned and readjusted his grip on the worktop, holding my head in place with his other hand and grunting with every thrust. As I felt him getting closer, he pulled out of my mouth and dragged me to my feet, lifted me up and carried me to the kitchen table, where we had eaten a few hours earlier. He pulled up my summer dress and yanked my thong over my feet. Sitting me on the edge and spreading my legs as wide as they would go, he sunk his mouth onto me. Instant pleasure coursed through me.

No man had ever made me feel the way he did. I was so

under his spell that I'd agree to anything while in this state.

As he teased his tongue across my clit, I tried to lie back but he pulled me back to sit up straight. I grabbed his head with both hands to keep myself upright, and to ensure he didn't stop, pushing his mouth harder into me. Shuddering with the intensity, I screamed out as I came, feeling his stubble rubbing against my thighs. Before I felt able to stand, he lifted me up and turned me around, bending me over the table and holding my hands together behind my back.

Seconds later, he was inside me, bringing my second orgasm quickly. With my face pressed against the cold table, his free hand was reaching into my bra and squeezing my nipple while he pounded into me from behind. I tightened around his cock as I felt him cumming inside me, panting loudly. He pulled out of me but kept me bent over with my hands held tight in one of his until his cum had run down my leg and was making its way onto the kitchen floor.

'Ah, Sass, I wish you could see what I can,' he said, his voice still gruff with passion. 'What a sight you are!'

I imagined him looking at my bare ass fresh from our kitchen session and was ready to go again.

He let go of my hands and passed me a box of tissues as I stood up. Feeling disappointed he hadn't gone straight back in, I put my underwear back on as he made our tea. We took it into the bedroom, and, as we sat drinking, side by side on his bed, he said, 'I would like to take pictures of you, Saskia,' he blurted out. 'Of us, so you can see what I see.'

The thought made me quiver.

'Would that be OK with you?'

I nodded, smiling. He was always finding new ways to excite me.

He pulled my dress over my head and picked up his phone.

'Oh, you mean now?'

'You're still wet from round one, right?' he said, gently patting between my legs.

'I'd love to photograph you now.'

This man really could get me to agree to anything. I nodded and grinned at him.

He spread my legs and stroked the wet patch, now growing at my crotch, and started taking pictures. I allowed him to position me wherever he wanted.

He took his time, moving my bra to gradually uncover my breasts between shots then working downwards. He slid his finger under the front of my thong and pulled it upwards swiftly, revealing my lips on either side. He clicked away, then removed it altogether, bringing my legs tightly next to each other.

I welcomed the feeling of my legs squeezing my twitching pussy from either side as he continued to take pictures. I eagerly waited for him to spread my legs wide to take pictures of the sight I loved him looking at the most; I was getting steadily wetter in anticipation.

Then he did it, slowly and one leg at a time, as he had done the night he cuffed me for the first time.

He expertly unhooked my bra and pulled it off, then stood there taking picture after picture. He rolled me onto my front and pulled my ass up in the air. He stood behind me and I couldn't see him, but the clicking had stopped for a moment. I lay there wishing he was back inside me, when, without warning, I felt his tongue penetrate me. Trying hard not to move from the position he had put me in, I let out a low growl, but as soon as he had started, he stopped again. I begged him for more, but he just gave my ass a sharp slap and continued taking pictures.

'I can't just look anymore, Sass,' he said a few moments later as I felt his cock slowly filling me up. I gasped and clenched around him, welcoming him back in. He fucked me hard, until I was sore, then pulled out and came all over my ass, taking more pictures before he would let me move.

After round two, we both cleaned up, then I fell asleep in his arms, my face in his chest. There was no other place I would rather be.

Friday night came around very quickly and I was in my bedroom putting on my new red lace Basque and matching French knickers.

I had searched online for days before going out to buy anything. Money was pretty tight with the shop and I didn't have much spare, but I really wanted to get something nice.

I had fallen in love with a Basque in Victoria's Secrets, but there was no chance I was going to spend that much money on underwear.

Having always struggled with money, I knew where to find the bargains. I sifted through piles of clothes in TK Maxx and there it was. Almost identical to the one I had put back in Victoria's Secrets, and less than half the price.

The doorbell rang as I was buckling my heels and I pulled my long coat over my outfit before opening the door to Jim.

'Right on time,' I said to him, giving him a kiss as I pulled the front door shut behind me.

I felt so much braver this time, ready for whatever the night had in store for us.

Jim looked amazing as always, in a pair of jeans and his coat done up just enough to cover his bare chest. I imagined what he looked like underneath and smiled to myself.

We got in the taxi that was waiting at the kerb and, half an hour later, were pulling up outside Gerry's.

As we got to the door, a different doorman checked our names and let us through. We were handing our coats to the cloakroom attendant when Gerry appeared.

'Hey, Jim, Sass. Lovely to see you back here. You caused quite the stir last time,' he said, winking at me.

I gave him a courteous smile and took Jim's arm as we walked through to the main room.

It looked just as it had last time. I thought perhaps some of the same people were there too.

I hadn't noticed the smell when we were here last. It wasn't an unpleasant smell. In fact, I quite liked it. A mixture of perfumes, drinks and sexual excitement.

I breathed it in.

As we waited at the bar for our drinks, Jim looked at me and shook his head. 'You look stunning, as always, Saskia,' he said, running his hand down the side of my basque that clung in all the right places.

'Well, you don't look too bad yourself, Mister.' Underneath his coat was exactly as I'd seen it in my mind. His jeans hung just below his hips, showing off his tan lines and letting me know he had no underwear on. I ate up the beautiful sight for a moment.

This time, we sat right in the middle of all the action and I noticed so much more going on around us. There was a dance floor, and people dancing. Not the dancing you would find in any old club. People were tightly pressed against one another, some with hands inside each other's underwear, some facing away from each other, and there was a woman dancing in just a thong. She was tiny and surrounded by three men, all in various stages of pleasing her while she moved to the music.

I watched without embarrassment, and, once I'd had my fill, continued looking around for new sights.

There was a man in a leather G-string kneeling on the floor with a collar around his neck. Attached to the collar was a lead. I followed the lead with my eyes and saw that he was sat at his mistress's feet.

She was scary; she looked like one of those bodybuilder women you see on YouTube lifting insane amounts of weight.

She was wearing a matching bra and thong, muscles bulging from everywhere and pecs where her tits should have been. Deciding that it wasn't doing anything for me, I looked around some more.

A young woman with long blonde hair caught my eye next. She was naked and stood against the wall with her hands cuffed to a bar above her head. She was beautiful. I let my eyes roam her taut body. Her skin was lightly tanned and her tiny waist moved slowly from side to side as she fidgeted against the wall.

Her special friend tonight was a George Clooney type with greying hair and a body that shouldn't belong on a man who was fifty-plus. He sat in a chair right next to her watching her while drinking a beer and occasionally leaning in to tease her with his hands or mouth. I watched them for a while, only stopping to look back at Jim, who was watching me intently.

We drank our wine and went back to the bar. Gerry sauntered over and asked how our night was going. He started talking to Jim and I tuned out, glancing back over at the girl tied up at the wall, her man currently bringing her close to finish with his mouth as onlookers watched. I felt a pang of jealousy; I missed it being me cumming for an audience.

'That's Jess and Rupert,' Gerry said, jolting me back to earth. 'Jess loves an audience as much as you do.' He smirked and adjusted his unmistakably growing bulge. 'I'll introduce you when they are done.'

Gerry said something to Jim that I couldn't hear then he gave me a smile and walked away.

I looked at Jim for confirmation of what I'd missed.

'Gerry said that there are certain rooms where people can join in.'

'Oh, right, OK,' I said, falling into deep thought as we finished our drinks. It wasn't long before Mr George Clooney guy and his lady friend were by my side with Gerry. Rupert, like all the other men, was in a pair of jeans, while Jess was in a deep-red basque and thong. I stared a little, enjoying the fact that I already knew what she looked like underneath.

'Hey, Sass, Jim, this is Jess and Rupert. You guys will get on great.' Gerry smiled one of his dazzling smiles and left us to the awkwardness.

Jim shook Rupert's hand and invited them to sit.

'I'll get us some drinks,' I said, standing up quickly so I wouldn't be left alone with the two newcomers.

I walked over to the bar and got another bottle of wine and two extra glasses and took them back to the table.

Jim was chatting to them casually, and, to my surprise, they were lovely and just regular people. I'm not sure what I expected. I mean, Jim and I were nice, normal people and we were here.

'Is this your first time here?' Jess asked.

'No, we have been here once before,' I told her, flushing a little as I recalled the memories again.

'Did you get to the booths at all last time?' Rupert asked.

'Uh, yes, we did,' I said, unable to conceal my smile.

Jim stroked my leg under the table and I uncrossed my legs.

'I like the booths,' Jess said grinning. 'They are always fun.'

The table went quiet for a moment, but, instead of awkwardness, there was nothing but sexual tension between us all.

'We are going to head over there now,' Rupert said confidently, standing up and holding his hand out to Jess, who stood up next to him.

'Join us if you like.' She smiled as they turned and walked away.

I looked at Jim for an answer.

'It's totally your call, Sass.'

This was it. I felt quite sure that Rupert and Jess were the right people to join forces with, so to speak. I smiled at him and got up. Jim jumped to his feet and followed me.

We walked down the corridor and I noticed for the first time that on one side were rooms for watching – the side we had been on last time – and the rooms on the other side were open to participation. I wondered how I would have felt if we had picked the wrong side last time, without knowing. I also felt a little cross at Gerry for not explaining that to us. Had he wanted to trick us into picking the other side? Had Jim known about this?

My head reeled with questions, but they soon took a back seat as I looked into the next booth and saw Jess and Rupert, on the participation side, which set butterfly flutters in my stomach. I felt a tug in my core as I stared in.

There was no one else outside yet, just the two of us looking in. Jess was in just her thong again, already cuffed at the wrists, her small breasts looking perfect. Rupert was walking around her in a pair of tight white Y-fronts. The sight of his straining cock intrigued me and I wondered how Jim felt about it.

I looked up at him and he bent down and kissed my shoulder. I nodded at him, signalling I was ready to go in.

Jess and Rupert both watched as we walked in. Feeling like I had just crashed someone's party, I stood like an idiot, no idea what to do.

Jim came to my rescue, as always, and cuffed my wrists above my head, so close to Jess that our arms were touching. He kissed me, biting my bottom lip and sending shivers all over me. He stood back to admire his woman and traced his fingers over the lace of my French knickers.

I looked at Rupert to see that he was now watching me, not Jess. He looked at Jim, who nodded his approval. Rupert moved in front of me and slowly unclipped one hook at a time down the front of my Basque, letting my breasts spill out in front of his eyes.

Now just in my lacy French knickers, I felt his hands on me. They were rough and callous, yet still gentle. I guessed he was quite a bit older than Jim, but I was OK with that. He was definitely fine.

He stepped closer and put his mouth over my breasts; I gasped and pulled at my cuffs. I looked over his shoulder to see Jim watching this man touch his woman. He looked like he was enjoying the show, allowing me to relax a little.

Rupert moved his mouth down south and I felt his breath

on me through the lace. He ran his tongue up my upper thighs and across to my already soaked mound. I groaned and pushed my hips toward him. At that point, I felt Jess move next to me, and, when I glanced over, I saw Jim walking toward her. I pulled at my cuffs again, this time in a protest to stop Jim touching her, but realised how pointless it was and also how selfish.

I couldn't expect Jim to be fine about Rupert's hands and mouth all over me but just sit and watch...again. And this was my suggestion. I closed my eyes and tried to concentrate on Rupert's expert tongue, and it wasn't so hard to do – until I heard Jess' breathing quicken.

My eyes sprang open again in time to see Jim sucking on her nipple and moving his hand into her thong.

Horror instantly raised its head, but, as I watched him pleasing her, he caught my eye and I saw the one thing that was missing. He smiled at me, but there was no sparkle. That was reserved for me.

The more I watched him get to work, the easier it was until I realised I was enjoying the view. I knew he was mine and I was his but it did feel strangely nice to share a little.

Rupert must have noticed my absence from our little scene as he roughly pulled my knickers around my ankles and plunged his tongue inside me, bringing my mind straight back to my own pleasure. The sight must have been glorious: two women, helplessly cuffed by the wrists with two beautiful men kneeling in front of them, working their mouths for our absolute pleasure.

Rupert uncuffed my wrists and took me over to the bed in the middle of the room. As we walked over, I noticed we had quite a few people outside watching. He laid me on one side of the bed and pulled his pants off, his cock springing to life. He was quite a bit smaller than Jim, which made me feel better for some reason.

He stood next to the bed and held his dick out, rubbing it on my lip. I rolled onto my side, opened up and took him in, repaying him back for my oral.

His dick felt alien in my mouth, and yet it all fitted so easily. I did some good work which clearly worked for him, but kept my best for Jim. Rupert was clearly close and was very loud.

Jim and Jess appeared at the other side of the bed and Jess laid next to me. She reached over and cupped my breast from behind. Rupert pulled away from me and walked over to Jess

Seconds later, my man was in front of me, that beautiful big cock close enough to eat. I hungrily sucked on him, struggling to fit it all in.

Rupert was now lying next to Jess and fucking her hard from behind, although she was watching Jim fucking my mouth.

Rupert reached over Jess and between my legs, finding my clit and rubbing little circles. I let out a low moan against Jim's cock and he grabbed my nipple between his finger and thumb and squeezed. Jim pulled out and stood me up next to the bed. He turned me to face Jess and Rupert then cuffed my wrists to a bar above the bed that I hadn't even noticed was there.

He pushed himself into me from behind and I growled with pleasure. Rupert and Jess were also moving. He had her on all fours with her face at my crotch and was kneeling behind her going for gold. Jess got closer and closer to me, until her mouth was on me sucking my clit and banging her mouth against me every time Rupert thrust himself into her.

I threw my head back against Jim's chest and groaned loudly. The door handle clicked and we all looked up as Gerry entered the room. Rupert backed away from Jess, letting Gerry in on the action. Gerry pulled his dick out and rammed it into Jess. Her tongue froze for a moment as she took him in but as Gerry sped up behind her, so did her tongue on me. I was so close; the sensation of Jess on me and Jim's hardness hitting my G spot deep inside me, coupled with our audience, had me on the edge.

I closed my eyes and let it wash over me, feeling both my breasts cupped and squeezed as I came, hard. I looked down to see Gerry watching me as he pulled on my nipples. Gerry looked up at Jim and he pulled out of me, moving around to face me. He kissed me and whispered in my ear, 'Can Gerry play?' I nodded, still a little unsure but not wanting to say no to him. Gerry uncuffed me and laid me on the bed. He pulled my legs open and put his mouth on me.

He must have done this to so many women; he knew exactly what to do.

He quickly brought me to the most intense orgasm I had ever had through oral sex; I couldn't help my cries of pleasure. As soon as he stopped, I felt embarrassed and violated. There was something about him that I didn't like.

Jim was next to me, lifting me onto his lap on the bed, facing him. He slid into me, but, as he did, he held me so tightly, like he knew what I was feeling but didn't want to let on to anyone else.

Or maybe he was claiming me back.

He pulled me down hard as he thrust up inside me, so deep, it felt like he was in my stomach. He filled me up with his milky, warm cum and kissed my head, whispering that he loved me.

Jess was still on all fours on the bed with Rupert behind her, fucking her for all he was worthwhile Gerry, who had been balls deep in her mouth, was now cumming over her face, but he was looking at me, smiling and giving me a wink. There really was something about him that unnerved me.

Jim wrapped me in a robe and led me out of the room, his arm protectively around my shoulders.

He led me towards the bathrooms and told me he'd meet me outside. I went into the ladies and quickly cleaned up, not wanting to be away from Jim.

I opened the bathroom door and came face to face with Gerry. 'Hey, you,' he said in a sickening tone. 'How are you feeling now, babe?'

I am not your babe, I thought as I politely told him I was fine. I looked around anxiously, but Jim was nowhere to be seen. 'I'm glad you guys hit it off with Jess and Rupert,' he continued, cornering me. I nodded, desperate to get away. He put his hand on the wall, blocking me from leaving. 'I'd like to get my cock inside that tight little pussy of yours,' he said through gritted teeth.

'I'm not sure I—'

'Oh I saw how crazy I made you, Sass, just with my mouth, imagine what else I could do for you,' he said.

I was unable to speak to protest, which allowed him to continue. 'I have had so many women that have come through here, but you... You are something else. Be my queen, Saskia, you know you want more.' He moved forward and kissed me, holding my arms at my sides.

I struggled against him, trying to turn my face away, but he wouldn't stop. He was so strong and had me pinned against the wall.

Then, suddenly, he was gone, being dragged away from me.

Before I could understand what was happening I saw a flash of Jim's face. I had never seen him so angry. He held Gerry against the wall and punched him hard in the face. I heard Jim telling him that if he ever touched me again, he would break more than his nose.

'Get the fuck out of my club!' Gerry shouted, holding his nose as it bled. 'You and that whore are banned from here!'

'Fine by us!' Jim called over his shoulder as he rushed over to me and led me outside. Minutes later, my coat was wrapped around me and we were out in the driveway.

'I am so sorry, Saskia,' Jim was saying over and over again. 'Are you OK?'

I nodded, so glad to have him by my side once more.

'I can't believe that prick!' I heard a woman's voice say. I looked up and saw Jess and Rupert stood with us. Jess came and put her arm around my shoulder and Rupert gave Jim his coat.

'There's a little pub just round the corner if you guys want a coffee?' Rupert suggested.

Jim looked at me.

'Saskia, what would you like to do?'

'Some coffee would be good,' I replied, feeling overwhelmed by kindness.

We sat in the pub drinking coffee until midnight. It was practically empty and the music was low enough to talk.

We laughed and chatted with our newfound friends, finding out that they were a couple and had been together for two years now and had been visiting Gerry's place for the last six months.

Jess told me that Gerry had always made her feel uncomfortable and Rupert got cross with her, saying she should have told him.

They were so lovely and I felt like we'd known them forever.

Silence filled our little table for the first time. 'Thank you, guys,' I said. 'This was just what I needed.'

The pub staff started to clear up and we made our way out into the night and called for taxis.

As we waited for the cars to arrive, I looked up and noticed how clear the sky was. The more I looked, the more stars appeared.

We exchanged numbers and vowed to meet up again soon.

Jim held me all the way home, apologising constantly for leaving me alone long enough for that to happen. I assured him that I was fine and that it wasn't his fault. We went straight into bed and, feeling exhausted, I fell asleep, safe in the arms of my man.

Chapter 15

I woke Saturday morning to Jim's soft breathing. He was still asleep and looked so beautiful. I lifted the covers to see that, as usual, he was sleeping naked. Like any man, his dick was awake before him.

I licked my lips as I stared at his morning glory. And glorious it definitely was!

Being careful not to wake him before I was ready, I slowly moved down the bed, pulling the covers over me until I was at his waist, then slid my mouth over his head. He jumped awake and inhaled sharply. He pulled the cover back and smiled down at me as I sucked him in, over and over again, rubbing my thumb over his head in between mouthfuls.

He groaned as I gripped his shaft tight, not letting up until his balls tightened and he emptied his warm, salty cum in my mouth. I swallowed it down and attempted to get up, heading for the bathroom. He pulled me back to the bed and buried my face in the pillow, arse up.

He started at my clit and worked his tongue up to my ass, licking and sucking all the way. Shuddering with pleasure, I came for him.

He produced a small bottle from the bedside drawer and took it to the other end of the bed with him.

'Tell me if you want me to stop, Saskia.'

I nodded. The gel from the bottle felt cold, but warmed quickly as it mixed with my recent climax.

He seductively smeared it around my tight hole, slipping his finger in gently. He rubbed the tip of his cock against it and gently pushed in, a little at a time.

I gasped as he stretched me, pushing himself in further. He slowly fucked my arse, stopping every time I pulled away. He moaned in my ear as I gripped him inside me.

His hands reached around and found my swollen clit, rubbing circles and bringing me to my finish. Getting off on my pleasure, he pulled out and came all over my arse.

He disappeared for a few seconds, then he was back to clean me up. 'I'm so sorry for that prick, Saskia,' he said, looking concerned.

'Hey, I'm fine. I promise.' I told him, 'And it wasn't your fault.' He didn't look convinced.

'I shouldn't have left you alone.' He shook his head and looked down at his hands.

I pulled him into me and held him tightly. 'You can't be with me every second. And you certainly rescued me from him.' I laughed, recalling Gerry's broken nose.

We walked into work, stealing a kiss at the shop door.

Jenny and I had a busy Saturday.

I told her about the convention I was attending – which was now only two weeks away – and explained what the weekend would be like. She helped me triple-check my orders and ensure everything was in place.

Jenny was going to go far. She really had her head screwed on right and seemed to be a very pleasant kid. She was quite tall and slim and had shoulder length blonde hair and big blue eyes. She was very natural and never seemed to wear any make up. Not that she needed it. She was pretty in a very simple way.

'So, how's your hot boyfriend?' she asked, looking a little playful.

'Ah, he's great,' I replied, trying but failing to hide my smile.

'I bet he is.' She squealed with girlish delight.

She told me about a boy she had been seeing and showed me a picture of him on Instagram.

She gushed over him, telling me all about him, then started to redden.

'He wants to have sex,' she blurted out. Jenny was eighteen and was a pretty girl.

'But you don't?'

'Well, it's not something I've done before, and it's kind of a big thing.' She shifted uncomfortably in her seat, avoiding eye contact.

'Jenny, it really is a big thing.' I said. 'Don't give that away until you *are* ready.' She looked up at me.

'You don't think I'm some weirdo frigid?'

'Not at all.'

I smiled at her. 'I think that people give it up all too quickly.'

She returned my smile.

'I told him I didn't think I was ready,' she said and I could see her processing it in her mind as she told me. 'He said that was OK and that he really liked me so would wait.'

I patted her arm. 'He sounds like a good man.'

I remembered my first time and how awkward and uncomfortable it was. At fifteen years old, I recalled wondering why anyone actually wanted to go through that and vowing that I would never have sex again.

Fortunately, the second time was with a guy who wasn't just in it for himself and had given me my first oral sex.

It had been the most intense experience of my life up until that point. And, after that, I did everything I could to ensure I gave the best head possible, so he always looked after me in return.

We spent the rest of the afternoon chatting in between customers and I hoped that our conversation had put her mind at rest.

Soon enough I was telling her to get off home and getting ready to close up. I was meeting Matt at Freddie's bar for a few beers.

Matt was sat at the bar chatting to the barmaid when I walked in. He looked different. More like himself than I'd seen him in a while. I watched him for a minute before he saw me.

He was so confident and comfortable with himself. The pretty barmaid was hanging on his every word, twirling her hair and beaming at him. I smiled to myself, detecting that his broken heart was on the mend.

'Hey!' he greeted me, smiling as I walked over to him. I grinned as he wrapped me in one of his bear hugs, then set me down on the stool next to him. The barmaid looked a little put out as she poured me a glass of wine, then walked away.

'Ah shit, did I just ruin something beautiful?' I said, nodding my head in the direction she stood.

'Ah, nah,' he said, shaking his head. 'Just a little chat while I was waiting for you.'

'So I paid a visit to that club,' he said, smiling.

'Did you?' I asked, laughing. 'And?'

'Ah, Sass, it was awesome! Rebound is always the best way over a breakup, right?' he said, laughing.

He told me all about his night, where he had ended up in a 'join-in room' with some hot blonde, then had another two women coming in to join the fun. He seemed like a new man. I listened intently, then gave him a lowdown of how my night there had been.

'Fuck, Sass, you OK?'

'Yeah, I'm fine. The look on his face when Jim broke his nose was priceless.' I laughed. 'We may need to find a new club though,' I added.

We ordered chicken wings, chips and onion rings and chatted all evening before walking home.

Sunday morning came around and I wandered into the gym feeling sleepy. After a good cardio session, I decided to spend some time in the pool but ended up mostly sitting in the steam room. I showered and dressed and got back in the car.

I'd texted Beth to see if she was around that evening for a catch-up.

Hey, yeah, overdue a catch-up.

I texted a reply to her.

I'm cooking dinner, Matt is home too.

She replied straightaway saying that she was in.

I started the car and made my way home, stopping at the supermarket to pick up ingredients for a Sunday lunch.

The three of us sat around the table eating roast chicken with all the trimmings. It had been a group effort and we had done well.

'So, not long now until your convention,' Beth said.

'Yes, next weekend. I'm praying it will go well. Could really do with things picking up.'

'I'm ready to do some selling,' announced Matt.

I smiled at his commitment. 'Good to hear that, Matt!'

Monday morning arrived all too quickly and it would be a busy week getting ready for the convention. I was seeing Jim Wednesday evening, but, other than that and lunches, it would be a long week without him.

The deli was getting busier by the day. Jim had recently started looking for some help as his customers had almost doubled and he just didn't have the manpower to do it all himself anymore. It was as if our little town had just fallen onto the map.

I wondered if I would ever be in a position to employ someone.

People who wanted actual books seemed to be a dying breed. Everyone had a kindle these days, or a tablet they could download a book onto and read wherever they were.

Still, in my opinion, you could never replace the smell or feel of a real book.

Chapter 16

The first half of the week flew by in a whirlwind of work and domestic chores, bringing me to my favourite part of my life...an evening with Jim.

I'd packed to stay the night as we wanted to make the most of it. I was just about to ring the bell when he opened the door. He still took my breath away every time. In casual jeans and a white t-shirt, I mentally gobbled him up.

'Hey, you,' he said, kissing me on the doorstep. I smiled as I crossed the threshold into his beautiful apartment.

He closed the door and backed me up against the wall.

Memories of our first rampant fuck came flooding back.

I thought about how far we had come as his tongue invaded my mouth and his hands undid my jeans. He pushed my jeans over my hips and around my thighs holding my legs together and got to his knees, licking and sucking at my clit.

What a welcome, I thought as I thrust my hips forward, getting close. Clearly reading the signs, he stopped abruptly and stood up. He kissed me again and grinned at me, a glint in his eyes.

'Let's eat,' he said, smirking at me as he walked away, leaving me in a state of desperation as I sulkily pulled up my jeans and followed him to the kitchen.

With my crotch still throbbing from my almost orgasm, I gave in and ate the beautiful meal prepared and served by my beautiful man.

Once we had finished, he cleared away the plates and I got up to help him load them into the dishwasher.

He put in the tablet and closed the door, starting the wash cycle, then turned to face me; the twinkle still hadn't left his eyes.

My jeans were undone once again and this time his hands delved inside, plunging his fingers deep inside me, massaging my G-spot as he caressed my breasts through my top. My mind on nothing but my incoming release, I leaned back on the counter, moaning.

Once again, just as I was about to tip over the edge, he stopped.

'Homemade apple pie for dessert,' he said, washing his hands in the sink and placing two bowls on the table.

I shook my head at him. 'What are you doing to me?' I said, exasperated.

'But you love my apple pie,' he replied, raising one eyebrow playfully.

I had never eaten so quickly as I did that pie, the pressure building up inside of me like I would explode.

He cleared away the bowls once more and switched the kettle on before sitting back at the table.

'So are you ready for the weekend?' he enquired, as if we were just friends meeting for a coffee and chat.

'I don't want to talk right now,' I replied. 'Other things on my mind.'

'Oh,' he said, feigning surprise. 'Like what?'

I shot him a look that told him exactly what I wanted.

'Oh no, Saskia,' he said calmly. 'I want you to beg!' His tone caught me off guard and I remembered the night in his car. I saw how he revelled in me begging him.

'I want you to tell me what you want from me. And then I want you to beg me for it.' His voice was so deep and dark it made me quiver inside. I stood up and walked around the table to him, my legs like jelly. 'I want you to put your mouth around my pussy and your fingers inside me,' I all but whispered.

'I want you to suck me and finger fuck me until I'm cumming in your face.' His eyes glistened and the corners of his mouth lifted into a wry smile.

'And how much do you want me to do this?' he asked.

'Jim...' I started.

'I don't want you to... I need you to. I need you to now!' I was so hot with anticipation, standing in front of his chair with my jeans still undone, my sex swollen, in need of his touch.

'Beg!' he said, darkly. His eyes locked on mine.

'Please, Jim, please. I need you to make me cum. I can't bear this anymore,' I pleaded.

He stood up and pulled me up to stand, then turned and walked away. Practically running to keep up with him, I followed him into the bedroom.

'Undress, please,' he instructed. I did as I was told, in record time. He lifted me onto the bed, still standing, and produced a pair of cuffs attaching my wrists above my head to a newly installed hook on the ceiling.

'A little light spanking is fine?' he questioned, reminding me of the limits I'd given him at the start of our relationship.

I nodded my agreement, heart racing, and he took a leather flogging whip out of the drawer. He ran the tassels up my thigh, his face close to mine.

The sensation sent tingles all through me. He slowly continued their journey up over my hip and all the way up my arms. My skin goose pimpled and my nipples hardened.

Next he ran the whip across my breasts and lightly down my stomach, then around to my arse. He gave it a gentle flick that stung momentarily.

I gasped at the sudden change of touch. Walking back around to face me, he slowly glided the tassels up the front of my legs and up to my crotch, tickling up my slit. I moved towards the touch, looking for more.

He gave it another flick and it hit my pussy, bringing so much pleasure for only a fraction of a second that I pulled my weight down into the cuffs.

He steadied me and pulled my legs apart, my slickness surely obvious to him. Whack! I felt the whip hit my arse once more, harder this time but the pain gave way to pleasure instantly. He rubbed it gently with the palm of his
hand, soothing my skin. His soft hands were a delicious change. Then, while standing behind me, he leaned forward and whipped my pussy through my open legs.

My head fell back onto his chest as his hand gripped my breast.

Within moments he had dropped the whip and was back on his knees in front of me, eating up the juices he'd produced. The intensity of his teasing all evening came together like waves crashing on the sand, bringing down the world around me, and, as I cried out, cumming hard, he stood up and pushed into me, still fully dressed, just his dick protruding from his fly; not having not been touched all night.

My pleasure had brought him right to the edge, just needing my warm, wet pussy for mere moments before pumping me full of his hot sticky cum.

He held me there, supporting my body while he uncuffed my wrists, then laid me down on the bed.

'I love you so much, Saskia,' he breathed in my ear.

'I love you too,' I told him as exhaustion took over and I fell asleep in his arms, not caring about the sticky mess.

I woke an hour later, and, while Jim was sleeping soundly, crept into the bathroom and cleaned up, pulling one of his t-shirts on and slipping back into bed beside him.

I relived our evening, bringing it back to life in my mind. It was only half past eleven but our antics had worn us both out. The more I thought about it, the hornier I became; my thighs now damp at the mere memory.

I looked over at Jim who was snoring quietly beside me and decided to take my chances.

I wiped the wetness from my inner thigh and my stomach knotted at my own touch. I trailed my finger across my crotch to my clit and breathed deeply. Trying to be as silent and still as I could, I rubbed little circles, surprised at just how wet I was. Feeling a little more daring, I pushed my finger inside and up to my G-spot, rubbing my clit with the palm of
my hand. Barely breathing, I brought myself back to climax silently while he slept next to me, wishing my hand was his.

'Playing without me?'

I jumped and looked over to realise that he had been watching me secretly masturbating. I must have looked guilty. 'Sorry, I thought you were asleep,' I said sheepishly.

'That's quite OK, I enjoyed the show!' he said, grinning at me. I felt my cheeks heat up but he didn't seem to notice as he replaced my hand with his and brought about my third orgasm of the night, quickly followed by my fourth as he slid his cock inside me and fucked me, filling me up again.

Before I knew it, Friday morning was here. Matt and I had packed up the shop and our overnight bags into the rental van and sat having some breakfast before we hit the road.

We chatted away and sang along to the radio all the way there.

'So, I have a date next weekend,' Matt announced.

'With who?' I demanded, taking my eyes off the road for a moment to glare at him.

'I have been talking to this girl on Tinder for a while.'

'I didn't know you were on Tinder,' I said, shocked.

'Well, I avoided it for a long time but then one of the boys signed me up as a joke.'

'Oh, a joke,' I said, teasing him.

'It was!' he insisted.

'So how long have you been talking?' I asked.

'A couple of weeks. She lives about an hour away and said she wanted to visit, so we're going out for food.'

'That's great,' I told him, smiling.

Once we had checked into the hotel, we put our bags in the room then took all the stock to the convention space to set up.

We were both ready to eat so then went back to the hotel, freshened up and met for dinner. We managed one drink at the bar after food before turning in for an early night. We had a long two days ahead of us.

I got into bed and Face Timed Jim. It was hard not seeing

him for a whole weekend. He was lying in bed, looking like a god with the sheets revealing his naked chest. I wished so badly that I was there with him. 'Well you look good enough to eat,' I told him.

'I could definitely eat you right about now,' he replied, his eyes dark and brooding.

I pulled the covers down to give him a peek at my naked breasts and watched his smile form.

'I have forgotten what they feel like,' he said, looking sad.

I ran my fingers down and traced them around my nipples.

'Well they are soft and warm,' I told him. 'Except here.' I pulled at my nipples.

He shifted in his bed.

'They look glorious.'

I smiled at his compliment.

'Anything else you need reminding of?' I asked.

'Well, I feel like I haven't seen that arse for far too long,' he said thoughtfully.

I threw the covers off and manoeuvred my phone to show him my bum, just visible around the edges of my knickers.

'Just as pert as I remember.'

I moved the camera back to my face.

'So, uh, what's under your cover tonight, then?' I asked with a mischievous grin.

He lifted the covers and dropped them again quickly.

'I'm not sure I can show you,' he told me.

'And why not?' I demanded.

'Well, I've got this hot girlfriend and she wouldn't approve,' he teased.

'I won't tell if you don't,' I suggested.

'Hmm, OK. But don't judge.' He turned the camera around, threw back the sheets and I saw his toned legs beyond his boxers and his beautiful erection straining.

An involuntary grunt left my lips as I looked at him.

'He looks happy!' I exclaimed.

'He always is when I'm looking at you,' he replied.

'I want to watch you,' I blurted out. 'I want to watch what you do when I'm not around,' my tone changing from flirty fun to hot and horny.

Without saying a word, he ran his hand down the length of his shaft, the outline of his dick tantalising through the cotton.

He slowly rubbed up and down as I heard him inhale.

I watched intently as he pulled the waistband down just enough for the tip to peek out from underneath. It glistened with his arousal.

My body started to heat and I felt the familiar tingle between my legs.

He wriggled out of his boxers, freeing his hardness. I gasped at the sight. His hand was gripped tightly around it, moving up and down, slowly at first then speeding up.

'You want to help me out?' he suggested.

I moved my phone lower and stroked my slit through my knickers. As he continued to masturbate for me, I removed my underwear and spread my legs for him to see. Bringing the soles of my feet together, I balanced my phone against them to give him a better view and me the use of both hands.

He moaned softly and his hand sped up. I rubbed at my clit and pushed my fingers inside as he furiously pumped his cock. Pleasuring myself while watching him do the same was like having my own private porn showing. With two fingers inside myself and my palm rubbing away, just like I'd done the last time I saw him, I was close to my goal.

Judging by his moans and the speed at which he was now jerking his cock, so was he.

I was suddenly very excited about watching him cum all over himself; the thought delectable as it ran through my mind.

My hands quickened their work as I raced him to the finish line, both groaning and breathing heavily.

He won. But watching his hand freeze and his cum squirt out onto his clenched abs as his cock pulsed was all I needed to bring me to orgasm just seconds after.

I woke before my alarm Saturday morning, having not slept much due to panicking about over sleeping.

I met Matt for breakfast and he hadn't got much sleep either.

We ate the complimentary Full English and drank copious amounts of coffee, then headed to the venue.

The day started quite slow, but within an hour or two of opening the doors, it became really busy.

All types of people came through and we had secured a great spot so that the majority were almost directed straight to us.

Customers came in droves and we didn't even have chance to stop for lunch. So far it was the most successful convention I'd attended.

By the time the doors were closed, we only had a quarter of the stock left.

We had decided to go out for food and a few drinks that evening to celebrate the first day, so looked up the local pubs and bars and headed back to the hotel for a quick freshen up before walking over.

I had a message from Jim asking how the day had been. I typed a quick reply telling him it had been good and that we were off for food, then dropped the phone into my bag.

The little family run pub we had opted for was great. They offered homecooked meals and cheap beers on tap.

It was like most pubs I'd been in with low lighting and an open fireplace which was empty. There was certainly no need for fires this time of year.

We ate, laughed, chatted and drank until the pub was almost empty. The bar staff had started to clean up and shut up for the night so we split the bill and headed back to the hotel.

The hotel bar was still open, so we decided on another few drinks before bed.

On reflection, this probably wasn't the best idea; having both sunk enough beers over dinner. But both being a little tipsy, the alcohol fuelled our poor decision.

It had been so long since we had got drunk together without other company and we were both enjoying ourselves.

I glanced at my watch, 'Oh shit, it's nearly two!'

Matt looked at me, wide-eyed and looking a little worse for wear.

'Fuck! Is it really?'

We had another long day ahead of us with an early start so we came to the conclusion that it was most definitely bedtime! I fell into bed and plugged my phone in to charge without even checking it, beer and cocktails clouding my mind.

My alarm dragged me from a drunken sleep far too soon

after I'd closed my eyes. My mouth was dry and my head ached. I scolded myself for drinking too much as I stood in the shower and let the water cascade around me, healing my hangover slightly.

After drying my hair and putting on my face, I took two painkillers with a pint of water and went downstairs to find Matt. He was sat at a table for two with a coffee in his hand. Another cup of glorious steaming liquid sat across from him. 'Urgh,' I said, sliding into my seat and sipping my coffee.

'I second that,' he said, glancing up from his mug.

'Ah, we really shouldn't have drunk so much,' I said, stating the obvious.

Matt shook his head looking decidedly grey.

We picked our way through breakfast and were both starting to feel a little more human as we arrived at the venue. Realising I hadn't even looked at my phone, I pulled it out of my bag and unlocked the screen.

Notifications glared back at me. Three missed calls and four messages from Jim. I instantly felt guilty as I opened them up.

The first was a response from my message yesterday evening.

I'm so glad to hear it went well, Saskia. What are your plans for this evening?

The second had come in around two hours later.

'I hope everything is OK, I tried to call but got no answer.

The next around 11 p.m.

Please can you call me, Saskia, I'm worried.

Then another two missed calls later...

I've tried calling Matt but also got his answerphone. Please let me know you're OK.

Feeling awful, I pressed Call and he answered right away.

'Saskia! Are you OK? I couldn't get hold of you.' Jim's voice came flooding through the speaker.

'I'm so sorry. We just lost track of time and had one too many beers and I forgot to check my phone.' I apologised.

'Sass, do you want me to re arrange the table a bit?' Matt called over, not realising I was on the phone.

I covered the speaker and called back, 'Give me a sec, Matt.'

Jim was silent at the other end.

'Are you OK?' I asked, keeping my tone light.

'I'm fine, thanks,' he replied icily. 'I'll speak to you when you're back.'

Panic started to rise in me. I had only ever heard Jim angry once and that was at Gerry. This time his anger was directed at me.

'I'm really sorry you couldn't get hold of me,' I said quietly.

'I was really worried about you, Saskia. But you were just out getting pissed with *him*,' he spat.

I tried to apologise again and explain that he had nothing to worry about, but he asked me to call when I got home and hung up.

My stomach was churning. I hated that he was angry at me but was also cross with him for distrusting me.

'Everything OK?' Matt asked.

'Yes, all good thanks,' I lied, not wanting to discuss it any further.

'Yes, we definitely need to rearrange the display.'

I busied myself away from Matt, the threat of tears burning my eyes.

Sunday was a lot quieter, as it usually is at conventions. I left Matt in charge so I could pop out and pick us up some sandwiches. We needed something to soak up the remaining alcohol.

As we cleared up after closing, I was pleasantly surprised to see that we still managed to clear most of the stock we had left.

We packed away what little we had and got into the van. I texted Jim to say we were about to leave. He read the message but didn't respond.

While driving home, I told Matt that I would drop him off at the house, then go to Jim's to see him for an hour or so. I think he knew something was up but opted not to pry. My mind whirred with thoughts of Jim and how angry he was with me. I felt sick at the thought.

I sat outside Jim's apartment, trying to gather my courage to go in and face him.

I knocked the door softly and my heart skipped a beat when he opened it.

My beautiful man stood in the doorway, but his expression was not one I wanted him to wear.

He looked straight through me and turned away, leaving the door open to let me in.

'I'm so sorry I didn't check my phone,' I started as I closed the door behind me. 'But you must know that there is nothing between Matt and I.'

Jim turned around and looked at me for the first time since I'd arrived.

'Saskia, I was so worried about you. You were miles away, I couldn't reach you and all sorts of terrible things were going around in my head. I was going out of my mind thinking something had happened.' He shook his head. 'Then you casually tell me that you were just out having fun and getting pissed with another man while I was awake all night panicking.'

'I don't know what to do other than apologise again,' I said. 'But you do know there is nothing between Matt and I?'

'Do I?' he snapped.

I felt anger start to rise up in me. 'I have apologised countless times for missing your messages and calls. I fucked up! But how could you even think I would be unfaithful to you, least of all with Matt.

We have been friends for as long as I can remember and there has NEVER been anything between us!' I shouted. 'What reason have I ever given you to mistrust me?'

He walked over to me and was so close I could smell his aftershave mixed with the smell of his skin. He lifted his hand and touched my face. I pushed him away.

'You don't trust me!' I yelled.

'I do trust you, Saskia. I just... I was hurt,' he mumbled. 'I hated the fact that you spent the weekend with him and not me. And then, when I found out you and him were drinking...alone. I just freaked out. I'm sorry.'

He moved closer and tried to kiss me, but I pulled away. I was still angry with him for making me feel so guilty over this.

'Come on, Saskia, what do I have to do to gain your forgiveness?' He looked like a puppy, ready to take its punishment.

I loved this man with all my heart and fighting with him was the last thing I wanted to do. I was tired and emotional. But I wasn't a pushover. Although I had already forgiven him, I still wanted to milk this...just a little bit.

'Beg!' I instructed him.

'Beg for your forgiveness?'

‘Yes,’ I replied. He dropped to his knees and held my hands at my sides.

‘Please, Saskia. Please forgive me!’

I softened my glare and he ran his hands up my sides. I backed away.

‘You can beg for that too.’

‘Beg to touch you? Beg to kiss you? Beg to taste you? Beg to be inside you?’ My crotch quivered at his words and the image of him lying on his bed, dick tightly wrapped in his fist, cumming for me ran through my mind.

Seeing his chance, he pressed his lips against mine, and, powerless to do anything else, I kissed him back, running my hands up his back and into his hair.

I had missed his touch and my body came alive as he pushed me backwards onto the chair in the kitchen, pulling up my skirt around my waist on the way.

He sat me on the edge and I leaned back as he sucked at my pussy through my thong. All the anger and pent-up energy was at the forefront as he ate away at me, ripping my underwear off and pulling me forward, deeper into his mouth.

He lifted my legs and dropped them on either side of the arms of the chair, giving him full access.

His tongue darted between my clit and my arse, dipping in and out of my pussy in between.

He had one hand on my thigh and the other on his cock which he had now removed from inside his jeans, rubbing its length.

The sensation of simultaneously arousing these three very sensitive places had me right on the edge. I was so ready to cum for him. I hoped he would let me, I needed the release, and I needed it now.

His hand moved from my thigh and his fingers probed inside me, while his tongue continued its journey from my ass to clit and back again. As I got closer, I grabbed the back of his head and thrust myself onto his mouth. My orgasm was so intense I couldn't stop my legs shaking. He lifted me off the chair and threw me over his shoulder, massaging the moisture from my climax up to my arse as he carried me into the bedroom.

He stripped off his clothes and laid me on the bed on my side and spooned me from behind, rubbing the head of his hardness from front to back, lubricating me, before slowly sliding his dick into my arse.

It stung as it went in, quickly transitioning from pain to pleasure.

He alternated between each hole, groaning as he slipped in each time.

'What a choice,' he growled. 'Do I cum in your slick wet pussy?' he retorted while pushing deep inside me 'Or this tight, perfect little arsehole?' he added through gritted teeth as he invaded my arse again, a little harder this time.

I loved hearing him talk this way and pushed back onto him, gasping as I took him in further. He rolled me onto my front and I lifted my hips, allowing him as much depth as I could handle.

He committed to my arse and sped up, emptying himself inside me as I squeezed around him.

We lay together on the bed; he held me tightly and kissed my head.

'I'm so sorry, Saskia,' he said, squeezing me against him.

'I'm sorry too,' I said, kissing his arm.

'Let's not fight again, please,' I begged.

‘Never,’ he said.

‘We can just make up without the fight next time.’ I grinned.

Chapter 17

I had decided to go back home Sunday evening as I needed to get the stock back to the shop and return the van Monday morning.

After tallying up everything from the weekend, I was delighted to find I had made more than I would usually make in two weeks! Feeling really happy with myself, I practically skipped to the deli to get my lunch and give Jim the good news.

Jim beamed at me as I walked through the door to the deli.

'Hi, beautiful!' he called as I got to the counter.

'Hi. I have just finished counting up everything from the weekend.'

'Well I'm guessing it is good news by the smile on your face.' He laughed.

'Yes.' I giggled. 'It went really well. Definitely worth doing.'

'That's great news,' he told me as he wrapped my salad box and handed it over, refusing payment as usual.

He brushed his hand over mine as I took the bag, the feel of his skin on mine setting my fire alight as always.

'I'll give you a call later,' he told me as I left the shop.

I walked in through the front door that evening to a magnificent smell.

Matt was in the kitchen making his famous chicken bhuna. He called out to me to say that he had made extra and was I hungry? My grin answered his question as I went into the kitchen to set the table.

'I transferred your money,' I told him happily.

'It was a really good weekend. Thank you so much for your help.'

'Thanks, Sass, and it was my pleasure. I really enjoyed it,' he said placing our plates on the table.

We nattered as we ate and Matt told me that he had found a new club that we might like through a friend of a friend.

'It's about an hour drive away,' he told me through mouthfuls of naan bread. 'I had no idea it existed! It's worth checking out though, right?'

We both agreed that we wanted to experience a little more of that particular lifestyle and that we would arrange the nights we were planning to go so that we wouldn't have an awkward meeting.

I went up to bed and dialled Jim's number.

'Hi, beautiful,' he greeted me after only one ring. 'I was about to call you. I've had a message from Rupert. He has asked if we want to meet with him and Jess this weekend?'

My stomach did a little flip; I had mentally revisited our encounter with them quite a few times and longed to continue our little adventure.

'Sounds good to me,' I said, hoping my response sounded light enough.

'Great,' he replied. 'Is Friday good for you? I was going to suggest they come to mine and I'll cook.'

I ran through the scenario in my head and told him Friday at his was fine.

'I have found my new employee,' Jim said. I could almost hear his smile as he told me.

'That's great. Who did you chose?'

'A guy named Bill. He has been working in a restaurant for the past four years in Truro but the manager had to sell it and they are knocking it down to build houses so he decided to make the move to St Ives to be nearer his family.'

'He sounds like he has some experience then,' I said, relieved that Jim finally had some help.

'Yes, he seems really easy-going and a hard worker. Hopefully he will be a good fit.'

'When does he start?' I asked.

'Next week.'

'That's great.'

We chatted for an hour in which Rupert had responded to Jim to say they were both looking forward to it. After we said our good nights and hung up, I rolled over and fell into a deep, dreamless sleep, exhausted from the weekend.

I got to Jim's an hour before Jess and Rupert were due to arrive, laden with carrier bags of wine and snacks. I had been tasked with the nibbles and booze.

Jim had already finished the dessert; individual cheesecakes. The little glasses were perfectly layered with the biscuit base, cream cheese and strawberry sauce and topped with fresh chopped strawberries. They sat in the fridge setting while he finished off the main course of salmon, potatoes and vegetables. I put the wine in to chill and arranged the nibbles in bowls on the table.

'Are you nervous?'

He thought about it 'A little bit. It's strange bringing the club to my home,' he replied.

I poured us both a glass of Dutch courage and cleared away the dishes while Jim went up to change.

He appeared back in the kitchen doorway looking gorgeous as ever in dark-blue jeans and a simple white shirt. I had opted for a pale-yellow halter-neck skater dress, feeling the warmth of summer still.

We managed a second glass of wine before the doorbell rang.

Butterflies flitted around my stomach at ninety miles an hour as we walked to the door and invited Jess and Rupert in.

Jess embraced us both with a hug, then handed over two bottles of wine. Rupert shook Jim's hand and kissed my cheek.

Jess looked far more casual than I was used to seeing her.

She wore a frayed denim skirt that just brushed the tops of her knees and a pale-pink fitted button-through shirt.

Rupert also looked casual in a short-sleeved shirt and dark-blue jeans.

Feeling a little awkward, we led them through into the kitchen and poured them some wine. They both seemed completely at ease, complimenting Jim's apartment and the smell of the food. We all sat and started on the picky foods I had bought on the way over to Jim's.

As we made our way through the first course, the conversation flowed, reminding me of how easy it was to be around them and banishing my nerves. We talked non-stop through the mains and dessert, laughing like we had been friends for years.

I drained the wine from my glass again and realised we had gone through five bottles between us.

Jess told us that they hadn't been back to the club and had

no intentions of spending another minute there. I thanked them and told them about the place that Matt had discovered, realising that I hadn't even told Jim.

They all appeared very interested in giving the place a try and resolved to visit together in a few weeks' time.

'I'm glad there is a new place to visit,' Jess said. 'We have both really enjoyed our time there.' She smiled at me as she said it, sending my butterflies back into descent.

I smiled back, feeling coy and flushed as Jim stood up.

'You guys want to come through to the front room?' he asked, casually.

The three of us stood and followed him in and the guys settled on the sofa.

Jess looked around the large room, running her fingers over the books on the shelves. Not quite as much as a book nerd as me, his collection was more non-fiction

I went to join her as Jim picked up a remote and put some music on quietly in the background.

'I would love to visit your shop sometime,' Jess said, still focused on the books.

'That would be great.' I smiled. 'You enjoy reading then?'

'I love it,' she answered, looking at me now.

She touched my arm and ran her knuckles up until she came to my shoulder. She stopped briefly, then stroked my cheek, bringing her lips to mine and kissing them softly.

Over her shoulder, I saw Jim and Rupert comfortably lounging on the sofa while watching us.

My attention was torn from them as Jess deepened her kiss, her hands now at the back of my head. Without even thinking, I grabbed her arse and cupped it as she continued her tongue travelling gently around my mouth.

She pulled away and took both of my hands, leading me over to the armchair next to the sofa.

Before she sat me down, she unhooked the halter strap around my neck and it fell to just below my bra.

Taking her time, she ran her mouth over the tops of my breasts and gently lowered me into the armchair. Moving my dress upwards as I sat, she positioned herself on her knees in front of me. I saw Jim lean forward to get a better look. Butterflies had now been replaced with the tug of longing in the pit of my stomach, spreading to my groin.

She grazed her lips up my inner thighs and flicked her tongue over the edge of my panties, then pulled them to my feet and dropped them on the floor. I inhaled sharply, feeling heady. Rupert was now on his feet and making his way over to us, followed by Jim.

Rupert leaned over and eased my tits out of my bra, sucking on my nipples and making them stand to attention. Jim was focused on Jess for now, and, as I watched them, I realised that I didn't mind one bit. He had his hand up the front of her skirt, playing around, making her buck her mouth against my pussy as she licked and sucked. Rupert undid his jeans and pulled out his cock; it was ready for action from the show and I opened my mouth and took it all in. He moaned and took control, fucking my mouth while stood next to the armchair, twirling my nipple between his finger and thumb. I watched as Jim laid on the floor and manoeuvred Jess until she was sitting on his face. After stopping briefly to be moved, Jess was back, eating away at me greedily while Jim did the same to her.

Jess was close and the closer she got, the more erratically she devoured me. As I watched her cumming at Jim's expert tongue, I teetered on the edge for a few seconds then climaxed loudly.

Rupert pulled his dick out of my mouth and replaced Jess between my legs before I'd even noticed her get up. He plunged his tongue inside me, spurring on my second orgasm less than a minute after my first. He helped me up and bent me over sideways across the armchair, kneeling up with the chair's arm for support. I instinctively raised my arse and revelled in the fact that I was on display again.

I heard him rip open a condom wrapper, then felt him slide easily inside me. Jess appeared in front of me, naked, with her legs spread. Jim was behind her, wrapping his dick before penetrating her.

I leaned forward and ran my tongue up her slit, making her gasp. As Rupert pushed me forward, I got close enough to return the damn good oral she had given me.

Jim's fingers wandered down until he found my clit, rubbing just how he knew I needed.

The four of us, moaning and panting as we sucked and fucked, must have been a sight to behold.

The image in my mind, coupled with what felt like a football team's worth of attention all over my body, brought me to my final frenzied release.

Rupert and Jim came quickly after me but Jess, although close, was still going.

I sat up and brought my game up too, sucking on her clit while Jim slammed into her from behind. Rupert stood next to her and slid a finger into her arsehole. Within seconds, she was screaming and shuddering with pleasure as the three of us finished her off.

After showing Jess and Rupert to the main bathroom to

freshen up, Jim and I went into the en suite to do the same.

I wasn't sure what would happen after the fuck fest and started to feel a little awkward again. Jim, who had obviously noticed this, pulled me into a tight hug and told me he loved me, kissing my head.

We were first in the kitchen and Jim called out that he was making tea. They both accepted and we sat back at the kitchen table as if nothing had happened.

After waving them off at the door, later, Jim and I sat on the sofa and discussed how easy it was to be around them and how it really hadn't been awkward at all.

'There is something, though,' Jim announced, making me look up from my second cup of tea.

'What?' I all but demanded.

'Well, I was hoping I'd get a taste of this tonight,' he said, brushing his fingers between my legs.

I opened them as if he had commanded it. 'What's stopping you?' I said, immediately wet at the thought.

He moved onto the floor between my legs, as Jess had sat and consumed me.

Every inch of me was reeling with ecstasy as he inserted two fingers in my pussy and one up my arse for good measure.

I came harder than I think I ever had before,
thrashing around the sofa as I flooded into his mouth. He turned me over and stretched me open as he thrust inside me, so deep it hurt. I felt him pulsate inside me as he came.

Later, in bed, and as I laid there in his arms, I replayed what we had done that evening and tried to make sense of it.

How could I love this man so much and trust that he felt the same, yet both enjoy sharing each other so much? My head ached trying to find an answer. Maybe it just worked and there was no other answer to be found.

I woke Saturday morning to Jim nuzzled into my neck, spooning me and sleepily grinding his morning wood into my bum.

I pushed back a little to let him know I was awake.

'Good morning, beautiful,' he murmured in my ear.

'Good morning,' I repeated, turning to face him.

He kissed me and ran his hands down my thighs.

My body responded instantly and my hips gradually moved forward, connecting with his hardness.

He turned me back around and ran his hands over my bum and between my legs.

Gently he dragged his fingers over my clit and inside me. I gasped.

'You are always ready for me, Saskia,' he purred.

I thrust back onto his fingers, pushing him deeper.

He teased my G-spot, bringing me close, then his hand was gone.

Slowly he eased his cock inside me, pushing in as deep as he could get.

I moaned as he sped up, grabbing his hand and directing it to my breast.

He tugged at my nipple and breathed heavily into my ear, calling out my name as he emptied himself, sparking my own orgasm.

I showered and was getting dressed as he got in. I watched him in the mirror as I cleaned my teeth.

The hot water was starting to steam up the glass, but I could still make out the outline of his glorious naked body as he lathered up the soap.

I was dressed and blow-drying my hair when he got out.

I switched off the hairdryer and turned to him.

'I'm going to visit my parents next week. They would love to meet you if you're up to it?' I said, praying he would say yes.

He looked at me with a genuine smile. 'I would really like that,' he said. 'I just need to get some cover for the shop on Saturday.'

'Bill seems to be getting on really well,' he mused, 'But I don't think he's ready to be left on his own just yet. I'm sure Scott won't mind. He owes me a favour and has done it before.'

'Excellent,' I said, feeling really excited about showing him off.

'Beth said she will cover and Ben is going in with her. The two of them are inseparable,' I told him.

I sent my mum a message while I drank my coffee to tell her we would both be coming up on Tuesday afternoon and staying till Thursday.. I asked if she would prefer us book a hotel room and she responded saying we would do no such thing; they couldn't wait to see us both.

'So, do your parents drink? Can I take some sort of gift?' Jim asked, looking nervous.

'You can take wine if you like,' I said, touching his face. 'They both drink red. But you don't need to buy them gifts; they are going to love you!'

Jim went into the kitchen to make coffee while I finished getting ready.

I heard a phone buzzing and, as I looked down, I saw Jim had left his phone in the bedroom.

'Julia' flashed up with a picture of her smug face.

My heart sank, why was she calling him? How often did they speak? I nearly answered, but something stopped me.

The call rang off, then, a few seconds later, a message popped up from her.

Hey, sweetie, just wanted to check the plan for my birthday.

I stood, frozen to the spot. I wanted to scream.

My head was spinning as I stood, not knowing what to do.

My brain was still misfiring when he called from the kitchen,

'Saskia, your coffee is going cold.'

I glared in the direction of the kitchen and grabbed his phone as I left the bedroom.

'You forgot this,' I said, slamming the phone on the counter.

Jim looked up at me, confused at my sudden mood change.

'What's the matter?' he asked.

'Julia would like to know what the plan is for her birthday,' I said harshly.

'I wouldn't mind getting an insight either.'

His face fell. 'Saskia, I'm going to go and visit my parents in a few weeks. They have asked me to go and help them with some DIY at the house.'

'What's that got to do with *her*?' I demanded.

'We were just going to catch up while I was there, it's her birthday. We have been friends for a long time, Sass, and there's nothing more to it.' He stood firm on his response, clearly feeling that he was doing nothing wrong.

'So were you going to tell me this at all?' I asked, holding back tears of anger.

'Saskia, I love you. But I can't just forget about Julia. She's my friend.'

'I'm not comfortable with the two of you being together,' I admitted.

He came towards me and put his arms around me. I tried to move away but he just held me tighter.

'I'm not going to stop speaking to her. You need to trust me, Saskia.'

'Like you trusted me and Matt?' I spat back.

'Please don't be like this?' he said, trying once more to hug me.

'I'm going to work,' I said, pushing him away and picking up my bag and coat..

'Clearly it doesn't matter how I feel about this.'

'No, Saskia, you're not leaving like that.'

'You have no reason to worry,' he continued. 'I would never be unfaithful to you.'

I tried to push him away.

'No!' he almost shouted. 'I won't let you run off like last time. I should have trusted you with Matt, like you need to trust me with Julia.'

I looked him deep in his eyes and believed him. But it didn't stop the way I felt about the whole situation.

'I still don't like it,' I said sulkily as I tried again to push him away.

'You don't have to like it,' he growled, pinning me against his chest.

He bent down and kissed my mouth. I tried to fight him off, not wanting to be a pushover, but he wouldn't let me.

He pulled roughly at my denim shorts, undoing the button with ease.

'It will only ever be you, Saskia,' he said, eyes burning into me as he thrust his hand inside my thong and straight up inside me.

He was rough and angry with me, like he was punishing me for being jealous.

I stopped my pointless attempt to escape and gave into him, feeling quite cross at how aroused I was.

He turned me away from him and pushed my head forward. I grabbed onto the door handle as he thrust his rock-solid length up into me in one swift move.

I inhaled sharply as the pain turned to pleasure. He fucked me until he came, unloading himself inside me, setting off my orgasm as he did.

I stood up straight and steadied myself, then looked at him.

'Always you,' he told me, then turned and went into the bathroom.

This was one I wasn't going to win, I thought to myself as I cleaned up in the en suite. He wasn't going to back down on this.

I either put my claws away, or I lost him. I thought about how I would have felt if he had told me he didn't want me to see Matt anymore and decided that, yet again, I was probably overreacting.

Chapter 18

We walked into work together, as if nothing had happened. Julia wasn't mentioned; neither was next weekend.

The smell of freshly cut grass helped to lift my mood. Summer was in full bloom and the signs were everywhere. The mornings were light and warm and the colours in the flowers were enough to cheer anyone up.

I felt like a spoiled child. Sulking because I couldn't have my own way this time.

I tried to push the feeling to the back of my mind as I sat at my desk in the shop going through my accounts.

The summer months were definitely beginning and there were a lot more people coming into the shop. The holidaymakers came in, dressed in their flip-flops and summery clothes, sometimes fresh off the beach. Some just came in for a mooch around, but most left with at least one book, much to my delight.

I recalled my first visit to St Ives. My parents brought me as a child and I remembered, even then, thinking it was the most beautiful place on earth.

I nagged year on year for them to take me back and I got my wish most years. We didn't have the money to go abroad, but I didn't care. A long weekend in a caravan or B&B near the beach was all it took to keep me happy.

At around eighteen years old, I dragged Matt and Beth down for the weekend and stood back as I watched them fall in love with it too.

I started with a little one-bedroom apartment, overlooking the sea. It wasn't great; there was very little space and it was in desperate need of a new kitchen and bathroom, but the view made up for all of that.

Beth and Matt had been up to visit a few times before Matt got offered a job around forty minutes' drive from the coast. Beth was out of work and still living with her parents, so we decided to look around for a house we could all live in.

Within six months, we were in, and loving every minute.

I was in the kitchen making some tea for Jenny and I when she called back to me.

'Saskia, there is a delivery for you.'

'Delivery?' I called back, trying to rack my brains to think what I had ordered.

I wandered back into the shop, drying my hands on the tea towel as I went.

Jenny was beaming. Next to her on the counter was the biggest bouquet of flowers I had ever seen.

The colours were immense; bright-pink roses, pure-white calla lilies mixed in with at least another four flowers I didn't know the names of.

The green leaves stood out beautifully against the pink and white.

I took the little card and read it.

Saskia,

Always you.

I love you more than you know.

Jim X

I hugged the little card to my chest and looked at Jenny, who was still grinning from ear to ear.

'You are one lucky lady, Sass,' she said as she took the tea towel from over my shoulder and left me with my flowers to make the tea.

I typed a message to Jim.

Thank you so much for my flowers, they are beautiful. I'm sorry for getting so jealous this morning. X

The response was almost instant.

I love your jealousy almost as much as I love you. X

One of my regulars, who always came in on Saturdays, called hello to me as she opened the door. We had a cup of tea and a catch-up as she browsed for her next read.

Stephanie had been coming into the shop for the last year and had read an alarming amount of books in that time. Today she came in with a proposition.

'I have been thinking, Sass,' she began, blowing on her cup of tea. 'Would you be interested in hosting a book club?' She took a sip. 'We could meet once a fortnight. I could make cakes and we could have tea.'

'Would it be during the day or evenings?' I asked, definitely interested in the idea.

'Whichever would suit you best,' she said. 'I thought evenings might be better so it doesn't eat into your selling time.'

I agreed that evenings would be better and Stephanie said she would get the word out to see what interest we could drum up.

‘I can put it on the Facebook page,’ Jenny said, clapping her hands excitedly. ‘I would love to come, and I have a few friends that would love it too.’

‘That’s great,’ I told her. ‘The more the merrier.’

I sent a few messages around friends who I thought might be interested while I ate my McDonalds burger and chips.

As I locked up the shop, I looked up and saw Jim walking over to me.

‘Hey you!’ I called out, smiling.

‘Hi, Saskia.’ He grinned at me ‘What are your plans this evening?’

‘I was going to get a workout in at the gym and then a swim.’

‘You fancy some company?’

I told him that would be lovely and we popped back to his to grab gym kit.

Jim hadn’t been to my gym before so I took him in on a guest pass. I showed him around quickly and we warmed up on the treadmill side by side, then went our separate ways to workout.

I stretched on the mat and looked over to locate him. I sipped my water and watched him pulling the weights bar down, every muscle in his back flexing. Watching him work out was such a treat; I decided to try and convince him to switch here from his gym. If I ever needed motivation, this was it. Just watching him had my pulse racing.

At the end of our workout Jim walked over to me, wiping

sweat from the back of his neck with his towel.

'Meet you in the pool, then?' he said with a smile. I nodded and we went down to the changing rooms.

I peeled off my gym kit and got into my bikini, showering briefly before going onto the poolside. Jim was already in the pool and I slipped into the water next to him.

We swam for a while, getting competitive at times, then he suggested the hot tub. It was empty; the pool was really quiet on a whole as it was past tea time. It was generally businessmen in the gym straight from work, who had usually made their way home by tea time.

Membership there was my one treat to myself. It wasn't cheap, but I spent a lot of my free time there.

They had a great gym, tennis courts, an amazing pool and also held classes.

We stepped in and sat down, the hot bubbles up to my chin. Resting my head back against the side, I closed my eyes and felt myself relax.

Jim ran his hand up my leg and I opened one of my eyes and looked over at him. He had his eyes closed, but his hand travelled further up and across the front of my bikini bottoms. His eyes were still closed as he reached just inside them and pushed his fingers up inside me. I adjusted my position, breathing heavily; giving him better access, then spotted two guys walking over.

My face flushed as I struggled to contain my composure.

They got into the hot tub opposite us and started chatting. Jim looked over and smiled at me, eyes sparkling, continuing his probing fingers. The bubbles frothed furiously, hiding the placement of Jim's hands from view.

My pulse was racing; the fear of being caught was such a turn-on.

I let my hands wander to his crotch, feeling his hardness through his swim shorts. I rubbed him gently without arising any suspicion and we stayed that way, teasing each other for another few minutes until Jim suggested we go into the steam room.

He stood up with his back to the guys, concealing his erection. We walked over to the steam room and I opened the door. Jim came in right behind me, closing it tight again.

My eyes began adjusting to the dark, steam-filled room and I scanned around the benches, delighted to find it was empty.

Jim sat opposite the door, against the wall, and I sat between his legs facing away from him. He pulled up my knee against the wall and I steadied myself with my other foot on the floor. He ran his hand over my breasts and down past my stomach. Sliding his hands back inside my bottoms and straight back inside me, I let out a quiet moan, grinding my hips up into his hand.

I could feel his growing dick against my back and reached my hand around, pulling his shorts down to get to it. As the steam hit our skin, it beaded and ran down my face and dripped off my nose onto my chest. Jim kissed my neck and moved his free hand into my bikini top. The steam mixed with the intense smell of eucalyptus filled my nose, opening my sinuses as I climaxed at his touch. Jim looked up just in time to see a lady pulling at the door and put his dick back in his shorts as I moved to sit next to him.

We sat in silence for a few minutes, grinning to ourselves before leaving for the changing rooms. Unable to keep the smile off my face, I entered the ladies and got into the shower.

Feeling dizzy from our steam room encounter, I went into

a private shower cubicle and brought myself to climax again, wondering if anyone would be able to tell what I was doing by my silhouette on the frosted-glass partition.

I got changed as quickly as possible and pulled my wet hair into a bobble, rushing out to meet Jim. He was sat at a table waiting for me.

'I think you may need to switch gyms,' I told him with a naughty smile.

'I think you're right!'

We decided to go back to mine and have takeaway. Matt was home, so joined us for food. We all sat lounging on the sofa watching TV while stuffing our faces with Chinese. Matt headed up to bed and Jim pulled me in to lie against him.

'I have a question to ask you, Saskia,' Jim said, looking down at me.

I sat up to give him my full attention.

'I'm not sure how you feel about this, but we spend a lot of time together and... He pulled a key from his pocket.

'Would you move in with me?' He looked at me, those big brown eyes so beautiful.

I didn't exactly need to think about it for long.

I had been waiting my whole life to find him...the real thing.

Did I want to wake up to him every morning? Fall asleep next to him every night?

'I would love to!'

He grabbed my face and kissed me.

'I love you so much, Saskia,' he said as he put the key in my hand.

'I love you too,' I replied, beaming at him.

We went upstairs, got undressed and into bed. Jim lay next to me holding me close, kissing my shoulder. He leaned up on one arm and stared at me. What a beautiful sight this man was. He lowered his head and kissed me passionately. Without a word, he slipped out of his boxers and slid inside me.

He lay on top of me, supporting himself, and I held onto his biceps as he slowly thrust inside me, again and again until we both came together. I felt so close to this man. So in love and couldn't wait to start our life together.

Chapter 19

The sun was streaming through the bedroom window. Thank goodness it was Sunday.

'It's another beautiful day,' I said as Jim opened his eyes and smiled at me.

'Not as beautiful as you.' He grinned a cheesy grin.

I put my hand over my face in embarrassment, then laughed.

'Come on, I need coffee,' I said, patting his leg and getting out of bed. 'We have a busy day,' I told him as I put on my fluffy robe and slippers. At just after eight, we were sat at the kitchen table drinking coffee after clearing away the breakfast dishes, when the front door went and Beth called 'hello' and breezed into the kitchen.

I flicked the kettle back on, making sure there was enough water for two more as I heard Matt moving around upstairs. Soon enough, the four of us were chatting around the table.

'What are you so smiley about?' Matt asked.

'Well, I have an announcement.' I beamed. 'Jim has asked me to move in with him!'

Beth squealed. 'That's amazing news!' She got up and hugged us both tightly. Matt stood up and hugged me, then shook Jim's hand.

'I'm so happy for you guys,' he said, smiling.

‘So when are you planning on doing it?’ Beth asked.

‘Well, we were going to start moving things today as we have no plans and are away at my parents next weekend. Do you mind? I know it’s short notice. Obviously I’ll cover the rent until my replacement moves in and you get right of veto.

We spent the day moving my stuff and Jim cleared out wardrobe and drawer space for me.

I put my toothbrush into the glass next to his and stood back letting the excitement wash over me. I felt so grown up; I’d never lived with a partner before. This was a big step and the most beautiful place I had ever lived.

Jim arrived behind me, wrapping his arms around my waist and nuzzling into my neck.

‘So what do you want to do first in your new home, beautiful?’

I turned to face him and kissed him.

‘Well, we could always do what we do best,’ I giggled.

He lifted me up onto the sink in the en suite and stood between my legs.

‘Hmm.’ He smiled. ‘Does it go something like this?’ His eyes sparkled as he moved in and slowly kissed my neck.

‘Mmm-hmm, something like that,’ I muttered. He wriggled me out of my jeans and thong and bent down, pushing my legs apart. He sunk his mouth onto me. I sat back, manoeuvring myself in between the taps, resting against the mirror. With his fingers inside me and his tongue at my clit, he brought me to a quick finish then stood up and plunged his dick deep inside me. He held onto the sink, gripping his fingers tighter with each thrust. Over and over until I felt him cumming inside me.

After cleaning up from our first fuck in *our* home, we decided on a takeaway to celebrate. Jim popped the cork on a bottle of champagne and we giggled into the early hours.

'Hey, Sass!' Beth called as she waltzed through the door to the shop Monday afternoon.

She had come in so we could go over what her and Ben would need to know while covering the shop.

'Hi,' I said, looking around her to the doorway. 'No Ben?' I asked, surprised.

'I thought you two were one person these days?' I said playfully.

'Nope,' she said, brushing off my teasing with a smile. 'I let him go to work most days.'

I went over everything I could think of that she would need to know. Then we locked up and both went back to Jim's.

We had invited her and Matt over for a celebratory dinner before we went away for the weekend.

Jim had made a lovely dinner of salmon, salad and new potatoes and we had finished it off with cheesecake and a bottle or two of wine.

'I can't believe how amazing this apartment is,' Beth gushed as I gave her the tour.

'I know,' I said, shaking my head. 'How did I get here?' I laughed.

'Ben has asked me to move in with him.' Beth blurted out.

'Oh my God,' I said, turning to face her.

I studied the excited look on her face.

'That's amazing news,' I said, squeezing her hands.

‘I told Matt on the way over. I was nervous about how he would react, but I’m hardly there as it is, so I think he was expecting it.’

‘Ah, he will be turning it into a man cave before we know it.’ I laughed.

Once Beth and Matt had gone home, we cleared the dishes and finished packing for the trip; we were leaving the next morning. I couldn’t wait to take Jim home to my family.

The alarm woke us the next morning at seven. I lay for a while, tempted to hit Snooze, but then remembered what today was and excitement pulled me up from my bed.

Jim rolled over and smiled at me as I got up and went into the bathroom, turning on the en suite shower and stepping in. I lathered and rinsed my hair, letting the bubbles chase each other down my legs and into the plughole.

I finished and got out, wrapping my hair in a towel twist and putting on my towelling robe.

I was stood at the sink cleaning my teeth when Jim came in through the open door.

He stood behind me and kissed the back of my neck. He reached his arm over my shoulder and slid it inside my robe, groping my breast, squeezing and kneading, then pinching my nipple. With his free hand he lifted the back of my robe, which barely covered my arse anyway. He ran his hand over the curve and cupped it gently before giving it a slap. He pushed his hand between my legs as I opened them, willing him inside me. He rubbed at my clit just long enough to get my juices flowing, then, as I sat back into his hand, grinding against his palm, he pulled his fingers away and pushed his dick inside me.

Gripping my hips he gained so much depth his balls were

resting against my legs. Slowly, he fucked me over the sink as I spat out my toothpaste and attempted to wipe my mouth with the back of my hand. He grunted as he came close, finding my clit again with his hand. We both panted as he brought me to orgasm then pulled out, cumming all over my arse.

'Sorry, Sass,' he chuckled, 'that robe is going to need a wash.'

Within an hour, we had eaten breakfast, packed the car and were on the road. The sun was already high in the sky and promising a hot August day.

The heat haze rose from the Tarmac, making the road shimmer and blur. Summer was my favourite time of year, and this was going to be the best summer yet.

After a few hours, we pulled into the drive of my childhood home. I could see Jim was nervous so gave his
hand a little squeeze. 'Don't worry so much, they are going to love you!' I told him.

My sister was opening the car door before he had time to properly pull up. She grabbed my hand and tugged me out, hugging me tightly. Jim got out the other side and she ran round to him, eyed him for a moment, then, very formally, shook his hand.

'You must be Athena.' Jim smiled. 'I have heard so much about you.'

She looked up at him, squinting with the sun.

'That's right, and you must be Jim. Saskia has not stopped talking about you!' she said, rolling her eyes. Jim smiled as the three of us walked up the drive to the house.

My parents stood at the front door, both hugging me before turning to Jim.

'It is so nice to finally meet you, Jim,' my dad said, shaking his hand and patting him on the back.

'It really is such a pleasure.' My mum opted for a hug instead of a handshake.

Jim was perfectly himself around my family and they all loved him instantly. There were no awkward silences or probing questions, everyone just got on well.

After a beautifully cooked family dinner of cottage pie, veg and gravy, we sat on the sofa, chatting about anything and everything. My parents wanted to know everything and Jim was happy to oblige.

'So, Jim, Saskia tells us that you own the deli in St Ives,' my dad said, sipping his tea.

'Yes.' Jim told him, turning to face him with full attention. 'I've just been able to employ my first staff member,' he said, looking proud.

'That's great,' my mum chirped. 'We love St Ives. Saskia fell in love with it when she was younger, so we've spent quite a few summers there. We would love to come to the deli next time we visit.'

'You would be very welcome,' Jim told them both.

'So do you sell cake?' Athena asked with a serious look on her face. 'I love cake.'

'Yes,' Jim said, laughing, 'we do have some cake. Your sister has requested carrot cake too, so that's on the list.'

I sat back, watching them together. It was a wonderful feeling to see them all getting along so well.

'Athy, I've got something for you,' I said, getting her attention.

She looked up at me, eyes wide in anticipation.

I pulled out the signed book from my bag and handed it to her.

She stared at the book, then back at me in silence. She opened the cover and Emily Trevor's swirly autograph shone from the page.

She looked back at me, her mouth hanging open.

'Is this actually signed by Emily herself?' she asked.

'None other,' I said, nodding.

'Eeeeeee!' she squealed. 'Thank you so much.'

She jumped up and grabbed me, hugging me even tighter this time.

'You are very welcome,' I told her, laughing.

When bedtime came round, we changed into bedclothes and got into the bed in my childhood room. My parents had kept my room as I had left it. The four poster I had nagged them for was fit for a princess, with drapes tied at every corner and fairy lights around the bars at the top. It was a strange feeling, bringing my grown-up boyfriend, from my grown-up relationship into my teen bed. Jim took in the sights of my room, picking up pictures in frames of me and my school and college friends.

He continued to look around, smiling before coming to sit with me on the bed. I fell asleep easily in the arms of my man that night, feeling nothing but happiness.

We spent the next day sightseeing. Something I had never really done there. When it's your hometown, it's not something you do often. I must have seen some of the sights as a child, but everything seemed new to me.

We spent half an hour walking around the cathedral

before we walked the fifteen minutes to Exeter quays, browsing the shops then moving on as it was almost time for lunch.

Everywhere you looked there were people enjoying the sun. The local park was a sea of people.

We walked past a group of people sat on blankets. Two couples were laughing and enjoying each other's company while they watched three small children running around playing tag, then rolling around in fits of giggles as they got caught.

The tree blossoms had been replaced by deep-green leaves, beautiful flowers appeared around the trunks in full bloom and the air was filled with the sweet song of the birds.

A burger van had parked up next to the path and the mouth-watering smell of hot dogs and onions wafted out and filled my senses.

We couldn't resist the smell, and ended up with a hot dog each, covered with onions and mustard.

After taking in the summer sights of the park, we went back home in the late afternoon to change as we had booked a table that evening for a family meal out.

My parents had invited my aunt and uncle.. My family would use any excuse for a get-together and my mum's sister and her husband spent a lot of time with my parents and Athena.

We pulled up outside the restaurant, dressed to the nines.

We walked inside and were seen to our table.

The chef cooked our food on a hot plate at the table, creating amusing shapes out of the ingredients and bringing them to life as we ate and drank.

It had been Athena's choice of restaurant and it was a firm

family favourite. The food and entertainment was always first class and the atmosphere second to none. It was Jim's first visit and his face was a picture. I watched him and felt a tug at my heart. How could one man make me feel so in love?

After a lovely evening with my family and a few too many sakes, we said goodbye to my aunt and uncle, promising to meet with them again soon.

Back at the house, Athena refused bed even though she was falling asleep on the sofa. We managed another bottle of wine between the adults before making our way up to bed. Feeling a little tipsy, we fell into bed giggling. Jim rolled me onto my back and lay on top of me. He put his finger to my lips and shushed me as he silently penetrated me. We made quiet, drunken love in my princess bed, cleaning up afterwards and falling into a hazy sleep.

Thursday started with the smell of bacon wafting upstairs. We got dressed and went down to find a Full English on the table, complete with pots of tea and piles of toast. My family knew how to eat!

Jim complimented every mouthful. We spent the morning playing board games, then sitting in the garden and finished off the day with a barbecue.

After filling our bellies with yet more delicious food, we packed our things into the car and said our goodbyes. My mum had taken *our* new address after hearing the 'fantastic news' – as she had put it – about us moving in together. And no doubt would be at the card shop first thing tomorrow morning picking out the perfect new home card to post out.

Athena had dropped her formal handshakes and gave Jim a huge hug goodbye. She turned to me for a hug and whispered in my ear, as she did, ‘I like him.’ I grinned at her, then leaned in and whispered back, ‘Me too.’

We told them all they should come stay with us next and they agreed, saying they would book some time off work and let us know what date was best.

We walked back into our apartment and I started unpacking my things, putting a load in the washing machine along with my robe.

We ordered pizza and watched trashy TV, discussing how well the weekend had gone.

‘Well, they all totally love you,’ I told Jim happily.

‘They do, don’t they?’ he said, laughing. ‘They are great, Sass. I had a really lovely time.’

I had a message from Stephanie, asking if Monday would be too soon for the first book club. I messaged back saying that I was up for Monday and sent the details to a few of my friends who had shown an interest after posting the event on the shop’s Facebook page.

I stole a glance at Jim as he watched the TV. He threw his head back and laughed at the comedy duo.

He looked down at me smiling as he finally caught me staring and pulled me in tight to his side.

Resting my head on his shoulder, I knew there was no other place on this earth on would rather be.

Chapter 20

I closed the front door and walked down through the hallway, calling Jim's name.

The apartment was eerily quiet.

I checked the front room and the kitchen but there was no one there. I even tapped on the bathroom door but it opened as I did, to reveal its emptiness.

As I walked up to the bedroom door, I heard soft music coming from inside.

Something felt a little off, I thought, as I pressed my ear to the door.

I could hear a muffled laugh, a female laugh.

I threw the door open to see them together.

My Jim and that bitch Julia.

They were naked and I could barely make out who was who with the entanglement of limbs.

'What the fuck is this?' I shouted, but neither of them even looked up.

'What the fuck do you think you are doing? I shouted again, walking over to them.

They continued to fuck, so lost in their own world that they didn't even see me.

I was stood right next to them. I pushed Jim's shoulder and he looked up at me.

He stared into my eyes, but didn't break his rhythm.

'You are going to have to just get used to it, Sass,' he said, turning his attention back to Julia.

'I'm not going to stop.'

I screamed and hit him, over and over again, but they both laughed as they continued, their moans getting louder as I ran from the room.

'Sass! Sass, are you OK? You were having a nightmare.' He held my head on his chest and I could feel his heart beating against my cheek.

'God, that felt so real,' I said, getting my breath back.

'It's OK, I'm here,' he said soothingly.

You were there too, I thought, trying to push the awful picture from my mind. It wasn't worth the hassle telling him, as it would just bring up the same argument again.

I lay back down next to him and waited for him to fall back to sleep.

Once his breathing had deepened, I crept out of bed and put on my fluffy dressing gown and slippers and shuffled into the kitchen.

I made myself a hot milk and honey and took it into the front room.

The sun was just coming up and there was a perfect view from the window.

I sat and watched as the sun filled the room with deep oranges and reds.

I sat for a while, feeling too afraid to fall asleep and back into the same dream.

After nearly an hour, I gave in and took myself back into the bedroom.

I only had half an hour before my alarm went off for work

so I just snuggled in next to Jim.

I found myself yawning through most of Monday and still couldn't get the image of Jim and Julia out of my mind.

By the time I went to get my lunch, I was annoyed at Jim for being such a dick in my dream.

'You OK, Sass?' he asked as I took my lunch from him.

'Yeah, just tired,' I said, trying not to blame him for my dreams.

'Early night tonight, then?' he said, grinning.

I had stopped off at the shop on the way home to pick up some essentials, finding I was nearly out of my shampoo.

When I walked through the door, the smell made my stomach growl.

'Ah good, you're just in time,' Jim called from the kitchen.

'Tea is ready.'

I put down my bag and went to investigate the phenomenal smell.

There were two plates of spaghetti bolognaise on the table; they were so meticulously plated, I felt as if I had taken a wrong turn and ended up in Italy.

Little bruschetta garlic breads sat on a side plate in the middle of the table and two glasses of chilled white wine were poured ready for our meal.

We both sat and started. I was ravenous, pulling apart the garlic bread and dipping it deep into the sauce.

After dinner we tidied up, then Jim took my hand, wine glass in the other.

He led me through to the en suite and sat on the edge of the tub, turning the taps on, and pouring golden liquid into the running water.

Soon the room was filling with steam and the bath with bubbles.

He lit candles around the bathroom and stood me up, lifting my top over my head and undoing my shorts.

I let them fall to the floor and he eyed me up and down as I stood in my underwear.

‘These too,’ he said, tugging at my thong as he undid the clasp of my bra.

I slipped them down and kicked them off my feet.

There was something very nice about being naked while he was still fully dressed.

He ran his knuckles over my bare arms, then his fingertips across my stomach.

‘You need some pampering, I think,’ he said with a wink.

He sat me on the edge of the tub and turned the taps off. The water now almost filled the bath to the top and I was looking forward to getting in.

It wasn’t time yet though.

He stood in front of me and slowly spread my legs, giving him his favourite view.

He reached over me and filled his hand with bubbles, massaging them into my breasts.

The soapy bubbles felt soft on my skin.

Getting another handful, he brought his hands between my legs.

The feeling as the bubbles popped against my clit had me moaning, my head thrown back and back arching.

He watched me as he rubbed his hand on me until almost all of the bubbles were gone.

He wiped away what was left and got to his knees.

Instinctively I spread my legs as far as they would go as he inched closer to me.

I could feel his hot breath on me and was desperate to be in his mouth.

Very slowly, he licked the length of my slit; I shuddered and gasped at the feeling.

He did it again, but this time travelled back down and penetrated me with his tongue.

I bucked against his mouth and grabbed his head, fucking his face until I had my release, screaming his name.

He helped me up and into the bath, kissing me on the forehead and leaving me to my bath.

The water felt like a blanket as I sat down, slowly covering me and keeping me warm.

I lay in silence with just the candles for light and pushed Julia as far from my mind as I could.

I was beyond lucky to have found this man; I needed to let this go so I didn't lose him.

I picked up my book, which Jim had placed next to the bath and let the story take me away. Getting lost in a fictitious world was one of my favourite thing to do.

Monday evening had come around very quickly and Stephanie and I were moving chairs and tables around in the shop, laying out nibbles for this evening's book club. We had gone with crisps and dips and an arrangement of cakes and biscuits. The kettle had just clicked off as our first guest arrived.

It was a very successful evening. Fifteen people turned up, mostly friends of ours – including Jenny – but four of them had seen the advert online.

We used the first evening to make our introductions and pick our first book. Everyone was very enthusiastic and looking forward to our next meeting in two weeks.

I walked in through the front door and Jim greeted me with a kiss. We chatted over dinner about how the evening had been. I told him the first book we had chosen was one of my favourites – *Fen*, by Freya North. It was the first romance novel I had ever read and my romance genre journey had begun right there.

'Rupert called earlier,' he said casually. 'He wondered if we wanted to give the new club a try on Saturday evening?'

I had been looking forward to paying a visit to this new place and it seemed a nice idea to go with Jess and Rupert for the first time.

'Yes,' I answered, smiling, 'that sounds good.'

Jim nodded and texted Rupert.

Living with Jim felt so grown up. I couldn't help myself but smile as we sat cuddled up on the sofa watching TV. This was us now. In a real relationship, living together and being in love. I wondered what our future would hold. Would we get married and have a family? We had never really discussed those things. I thought about carrying our child and dismissed it quickly. I had never really been very maternal. I wondered if Jim wanted children. He had never mentioned it before. Maybe he felt the same as me.

My thoughts were interrupted by his wandering hands. His fingers pulled out my breast from my vest top as I leaned against him. My crotch tingled as he rolled my nipple between his finger and thumb. His other hand was lightly running up my thigh over my pyjama bottoms.

He got up, stripped me and pulled me to the end of the sofa, positioning my bum on the arm; he laid me back, my legs dangling over the side. He got to his knees and pushed my legs apart, gliding his hands up my stomach to my breasts and back down. His touch was so soft and warm. He lowered his mouth onto me, dipping his tongue inside me, lapping up my wetness as he did. He was licking and sucking my arse and clit until I shook with delight as I climaxed, flooding his mouth.

He got up and thrust his dick inside me; I squeezed around his welcome intrusion. He straightened his back and pulled me closer, his cock pushing deeper into me. He fucked me hard. I gazed up at him from the sofa; he looked glorious in the soft light of the lamp.

His arms flexed as he gripped my waist, holding me in place as he moaned with every move. He sat backwards slightly to get the deepest angle, giving me an incomparable view.

Beads of sweat ran down his beautiful chest and into the smattering of dark hair. His face was dark and brooding as his jaw clenched and he groaned a little louder, pumping me full of his warm, sticky cum.

Chapter 21

It was Saturday evening. The new club was just short of an hour drive away so we had booked an Uber. It was a pleasant evening, and, as we got out of the car we saw Jess and Rupert just outside the club.

We exchanged hugs, kisses and pleasantries as we walked to the entrance, confirming our places on the guest list with the man at the door.

It was a lot more modern from the outside than Gerry's place. When our coats were taken and we opened up the doors to the main hall, I was shocked at how much bigger and more spacious it felt inside. There was a big round staged area right in the middle of the room with people dancing on and around it. There were four different bars at each corner of the huge room and small open-fronted booths with slightly frosted-glass partitions lined the walls. The sounds of gentle moaning and excited panting filled the room.

We made our way to the bar in the furthest corner and Jess hopped up onto one of the stools. She looked beautiful as always. She wore a hot-pink corset and a matching, skin-tight skirt. As she sat, looking around the room, I could see she had stocking and suspenders on underneath.

Jim had picked my outfit for the evening and it wasn't too dissimilar to Jess's. Although mine, in a charcoal grey, had cutouts at each side, leaving skin on display and not much to the imagination in length. Underneath, he had teamed it with matching crotchless panties, this time without the pearls.

Jim and Rupert were both in jeans and nothing else. Jim's were light and ripped at the knees and were quite contrasting to the dark pair Rupert wore.

We all sat drinking tall glasses of chilled champagne and made small talk as we studied the room and its occupants.

'Apparently the dance floor doubles as a stage for extra public shows where anyone can join in,' Jess said, winking at me.

'Oh,' I responded, smiling at her. It was such an odd relationship between the four of us. I should surely feel embarrassed by it, but wasn't at all. It just worked.

I looked over at the booths. 'They look like fun, too,' I announced to the other three, who all agreed. They were much like the rooms at Gerry's, but the fronts were completely open instead of glass-fronted with a door. There were different props in each. From where we were sitting, we had a clear view into at least six of the twenty-four booths down the walls. Five out of the six were occupied and in full swing. I grinned to myself, getting my fill of voyeurism.

There were lots of different people in the booths, some with just one other, some with a few, men on men, women on women, mixed and even a girl on her own. She sat completely naked on a bar stool right at the front of the nearest booth, her legs spread. She had her fingers deep inside her, furiously rubbing at her G-spot and clit. She pulled her hand away and liquid ejaculated out of her at speed. She was screaming as she squirted out all over the floor. No sooner had she got up from the stool than a man, who must have been in his thirties, had entered the room and was pressing himself against her naked body, kissing her neck.

Jim touched my arm, turning my attention away and leading me to a table near the stage where we sat drinking for a while, finding our feet.

Before long, the music quietened down and the dancefloor started to clear. Within minutes, everyone was at tables with drinks ready for the show. We were front and centre, with a great view for whatever was happening next.

A very tall, leggy blonde with huge tits and a tiny waist walked up the steps onto the stage. Dressed in a black lace plunge bra and matching thong, she led a young man behind her. I guessed he was twenty at the most. He was wearing nothing but a G-string and was blindfolded. He looked uneasy and nervous, but didn't resist.

The woman pulled a large frame in the shape of an X up from the floor of the stage and locked it into place with its top points angled straight up at the ceiling. She moved the man into position, cuffing his wrists and ankles to each point. She ran her hands over his chest and whispered something into his ear. He smiled and relaxed a little. She turned around and began to address the eager audience.

'His name is Tom and he's a little nervous. He's never done anything like this before, but I know how much he will enjoy it,' she said grinning from ear to ear. 'Be gentle with him,' she added with a wink.

She stood behind him and ran her hands down his sides to the tops of his legs, then gave his ass a sharp slap. She bent over a little and stroked up the inside of his thighs. His cock stiffened inside the G-string. Moving her hand between his legs, with a quick tug, she pulled off the material freeing his manhood. He pulled at the cuffs a little and his breathing noticeably sped up. I imagined how he felt at that point; that his heart must feel as though it was beating out of his chest with excitement and nerves.

Still standing behind him, she squeezed his balls and ran the palm of her hand upwards, stroking his shaft from bottom to top and back down again. He thrust his hips forward, pushing himself into her hand and she forcefully pulled him back, then took her hand away and walked around in front of him. She stood at the front of the stage and scanned the crowd. She pointed at a brunette lady in the back row. The lady practically jumped out of her seat and ascended the stairs to the stage. She must have been around forty and was a little heavier than the blonde. She wore a pretty baby doll that accentuated all of her perfect curves. She walked over to Tom who was still blind to his surroundings, completely unaware of what was coming next.

The brunette walked towards Tom and got onto her knees. I wondered if he could sense anyone in front of him as she had been very careful not to touch him or make a sound. His dick stuck out at a perfect right angle to his body, stiff and desperate for more attention. Brunette licked her lips and put her mouth around him, taking him all the way in. He gasped and bucked against her, without knowing anything about her. She sucked him over and over while he moaned loudly until the blonde tapped her on the shoulder and she instantly stopped. He hung his head forward, seemingly unable to hold it up as the brunette made her way back to her seat.

The blonde was back at the front of the stage looking for more volunteers. She glanced over at our table and panic hit me. She made eye contact with me then looked over to Jess, beckoning her over. Jess got to her feet and started for the stage. The blonde looked around her and nodded at me too. I slowly got to my feet, butterflies circling my stomach. We got up to the stage and the blonde walked over to us. 'Give me a hand laying this down please, ladies,' she asked, gesturing to the X. She told Tom that he was about to be laid down as she undid a series of clips. Showing us where to hold, the three of us gently laid the X onto the floor.

It was surprisingly easy to do and glided gently to the floor. 'Anything goes, girls,' she whispered, slipping a condom into my hand 'Give them a show and him the time of his life! Don't cum too quickly,' she ordered Tom as she left the crowd to us. Jess pulled at her tiny skirt and it fell to the floor revealing a suspender belt and crotchless thong. She walked over to him and stood with one foot either side of his head, facing his feet. She slowly bent her knees, opening her legs wide until she was squatting just above his face, her pussy protruding from the straps of her crotchless panties.

She rolled her hips back then lowered herself onto his mouth, grinding forward as they made contact. Tom sprang to life, greedily eating at her pussy as she rocked back and forth, now on her knees. I suddenly realised that I was just standing like an idiot and should be doing something. I looked down at his young, naked body and admired his physique. His dick wasn't huge, but he certainly wasn't lacking. Remembering my little skirt barely covering my bare crotch, excitement flitted through me; I was desperate to be looked at. I glanced over to our table, where Jim and Rupert sat. Jim looked at me intensely, inspiring me to give him the best show I could.. I walked over to Tom and stood one foot either side of his legs with my back to the audience. I got onto all fours as seductively as possible, arching my back and putting my arse in the air. With my pussy and arse on full display, I put my mouth around his dick, licking up his pre cum. He gasped and groaned as I took him in.

I worked my magic mouth on him as Jess fucked his face, sounding close to orgasm. I felt Tom's balls contract and him pull away. Understanding he was close but wasn't allowed to cum just yet, I gave his balls a sharp tug and sat up. I let him rest for a few seconds to regain control then ripped open the condom wrapper and slid it over his dick, rolling it all the way down. Jess grinned at me and stood up.

'You need to try this tongue,' she whispered to me. The corners of Tom's mouth turned up into a smile on hearing this compliment.

'Well how could I turn that down,' I whispered back, swapping places. Jess was right, Tom may be young, but he was certainly very talented with his mouth. I sat down on his face rubbing my clit on his bottom lip and he eagerly sucked at me, flicking his tongue at my arse. . Jess sat down on his dick, her face twisted in sheer pleasure as she did. She sat forward and kissed me, reaching down my sides and pulling my breasts out to the top of my Basque.

She bounced on him, bringing them both close to climax as I rode his face. The three of us got louder the closer we came, playing up to our audience. I looked over at Jim who looked positively rampant, pumping his dick in his hand.

Scanning around the room, I saw that most of the crowd were also pleasing themselves or each other while watching the show. Jess squeezed my nipples bringing me back into the moment and we all came closely together, moaning hoarsely.

The blonde was back at his side, helping me to my feet. We pulled the X back upright and the blonde removed Tom's blindfold. He blinked a few times then took in the scene around him; his two pleasers looking sated and his audience horny as hell from the show.

His restraints were removed and he grinned at us both as he walked proudly off the stage, dick swaying side to side, still covered by his cum-filled condom.

We made our way back to the table to find Jim and Rupert on their feet. Jim put his one arm around my shoulder and kissed me deeply while he thrust his other hand under my little skirt, his fingers delving straight inside me.

'That was a real fucking show, Sass,' he growled. 'We need you both in a booth. NOW!' he ordered, pulling me closer to him with his fingers, which were still inside me.

Rupert and Jess were already heading towards the booths and I was happy to follow. We went into the nearest unoccupied booth and Jim turned a card at the front from green to red, signalling no one else was to join in.

There was a hospital bed in the middle of the room, complete with stirrups at the end. Jim pushed me onto the end of the bed and strapped my feet into the stirrups while Rupert sat Jess on the side of the bed and pulled up an examining stool in front of her open legs.

Both our men sunk their mouths onto us, probing us with their tongues. Unable to move my legs, I succumbed to Jim's desperation for me and lay back while he brought me right back to breaking point. Rupert had spun Jess around and had her bent over the bed fucking her roughly. Jim stopped and looked over at them, deciding that's what he needed; standing on the low step at the end of the bed, he rammed his rock-hard cock inside me, fucking me hard and deep and making me scream out in delight.

'Fuck, I wanted you so bad when you were up there, Sass,' he told me through gritted teeth. 'Watching everyone looking at you both was so fucking hot.'

Rupert nodded in agreement, unable to speak. Jess groaned and pushed back against Rupert's dick as they both came together. Jim thrust inside me again, holding his position this time, and I felt his dick throbbing as he found his much-needed release. He pulled out and watched as his cum trickled out of me and made its way down to my arse. He stopped it with his finger and massaged it into my arsehole for lubricant before slipping his finger in, sending ripples of sensation through me. Still on my back and unable to move my legs, I wriggled around on the bed, feeling ready to come again. Rupert appeared and Jim removed his finger, and stepped aside. Rupert rolled on a condom and penetrated my arse, moaning softly as he did.

Jim was at my side with his dick in my face. I turned and sucked him in, tasting the mixture of both of our cum. He fucked my mouth hard, taking full control and holding my hands above my head. Jess appeared and climbed on top of me on all fours, her breasts against mine and her arse in Rupert's face. He sunk his mouth into her again whilst balls deep in me. None of us lasted long. It was frenzied but needed; as if one session hadn't been enough to quite satisfy the level of horny we had all reached.

After cleaning up, we decided to leave and have a few drinks at the pub a few streets down. As always, everything was just normal and free of any awkwardness after. We laughed and drank and ordered some nibbles to share. It was a lovely end to an excellent night.

We waved them off in a taxi and got into our Uber.

'You were amazing tonight, Saskia,' Jim told me. 'Watching you up there on a stage in front of so many people was such a turn-on.'

I giggled. 'Yeah, it was pretty hot being up there,' I admitted. 'Better once I saw you sat there with your dick out, though.' I winked and nudged him playfully. He grinned back at me.

'Couldn't help it.' He shrugged.

Chapter 22

I laced up my trainers as Jim stood at the door waiting for me. Our new Sunday routine started with a run.

'Don't start without me,' I warned, jumping to my feet.

'Wouldn't dream of it.' He smiled, getting ready to run off.

I pulled the front door behind us and we walked down the stairs, opening the outside door to the street.

'OK,' I said, giving him a playful punch in the arm and taking off, running past him.

'Cheat!' he shouted as he sped up behind me, taking over as he blew me a kiss.

'You're not going to win!' I shouted, catching up.

Our runs had become quite competitive and I had lost last Sunday so wasn't going to let that happen again today.

We got back home – after managing to beat him by a couple of seconds – and I stripped off my clothes and turned the water on in the shower. Jim joined me, peeling off his top and shorts, sweat clinging to his chest hair.

The water felt cool and fresh against my hot skin. I closed my eyes and tilted my head back to let the water soak my hair. Jim lathered up the shower puff and gently rubbed the soapy bubbles all over my skin. As I rinsed my shampoo off he replaced the puff with his hand, massaging my breasts then turning me around, pulling me backwards against him until his semi-hard cock sat in the crack of my bare arse.

Keeping one hand on my breast, the other moved down between my legs, spreading my lips and sliding his fingers inside me. He quickly and expertly brought my climax about with four fingers inside me and his palm rubbing against my clit. Feeling my knees weaken, he caught me as I fell forward, the steam from the shower mixed with the intensity of my orgasm making me lightheaded.

He helped me out of the shower and wrapped us both in robes, then led me out to the balcony. Moments later, he appeared with two mugs of steaming coffee.

It was a beautiful morning with a glorious autumnal feeling. We sat for an hour, just enjoying the moment.

We spent the rest of our Sunday moving the last of my things from the house.

A new housemate was moving in the following morning so we gave Beth's room a final clean for him. My room needed a coat of paint before the second new housemate could move in and Matt hadn't found another person he was comfortable with yet.

'Paulo seems like a good guy,' Matt told me. 'He's our age and he's a doctor.'

'Wow, that's pretty impressive,' I said, wondering if they would have the same interests.

'Yeah, he's come over from Portugal to further his career and has got a job in the surgery here.'

'I'm glad you have found someone to take at least one of the rooms.'

'Me too, was starting to rattle around that house on my own.' He laughed.

'Well, I look forward to meeting him. I'll call over next week.'

'That would be nice, Sass, come over for dinner if you like?'

'Sounds good to me.' I smiled.

I opened the shop Monday morning and was just finishing my coffee when the bell above the door rang and in came my first customer of the day. I looked up to see a very tall, olive-skinned man entering. 'Saskia?' he asked with a thick Portuguese accent.

'Hi, yes,' I stuttered.

'I am Paulo, your friend Matt told me all about you and your shop. I have a passion for books so I very much wanted to visit.' I felt as though he was staring into my soul.

'It's very lovely to meet you, Paulo,' I told him, holding my hand out to shake his. He took my hand and kissed the back, looking deep into my eyes.

'The pleasure is all mine. Although Matt did not tell me how beautiful you are!'

I couldn't suppress the blush which coloured my face and looked away quickly. He released my hand and I turned away, taking his attention to the shop instead. I showed him around and asked what books he liked to read, desperate to change the subject and put some distance between us.

His soft accent affected my senses as he spoke of his country and the books he loved to read. We talked for an hour, connecting through our mutual love of reading, and, when it came time for him to leave, he pulled me close and kissed my cheek.

'What a pleasure it was to meet you, beleza.'

Having no clue what he had just called me and feeling dizzy

from his touch, I mumbled that I would be calling to the house later in the week. As he closed the door behind him, my phone beeped on the counter: a message from Matt telling me that Paulo might call into the shop.

'Nice heads-up,' I thought to myself as I responded to say he had already been in. I didn't feel that I should disclose my thoughts on Paulo or how he had affected me, so I just told Matt that he seemed nice and that I would be there Wednesday evening after work for dinner as we had planned.

As we pottered about the kitchen making dinner on Monday evening, Jim told me that his friend Scott was having some issues with his girlfriend and had asked if he was free Wednesday evening for a pint at Ed's. 'I told him I wasn't sure if we had plans,' he called over his shoulder as he chopped an onion.

'Ah, it's not a problem,' I told him. 'It's just dinner with Matt and his new housemate. I can go on my own, you go cheer Scott up,' I said, rubbing his arm as I walked past to get to the fridge. I hadn't told Jim that I'd met Paulo already. I was worried my face might flush, giving away more than I wanted. I breathed in a hidden sigh of relief that Jim wouldn't be meeting Paulo just yet. After dinner with him and Matt, I was sure things would be fine. I would talk about Jim all evening to ensure Paulo got the message.

I sprinkled grated parmesan on top of the carbonara Jim had just plated up and we sat and ate in silence, both contemplating our own thoughts.

After dinner, Jim poured us both some tea and we sat out on the balcony, just outside the bedroom. I'd put on a long satin dressing gown. I crossed my legs and let the robe fall open slightly, showing my bare thigh.

Jim looked over at me, the naughty sparkle lighting his eyes. He ran his hand up my leg to my thigh. It was still light out and our balcony was far from hidden, although there was no one around and you would have to look up to see us. He put his cup on the table and got to his knees, pulling me to the edge of my chair and opening my robe.

I moaned as he put his mouth on me; the sensation of his tongue lightly trailing over me was exquisite. He undid the belt and pulled the gown fully open, letting it fall to my sides.

Now sitting back in the garden chair, I revelled in the breeze blowing around my naked skin as he sucked at me. After my first orgasm, he sat on the chair, releasing his dick from his lounge pants, and lifted me onto it, facing out into the street. Luckily we were a two floors up as there was now a couple walking below us. He playfully covered my mouth as he bounced me up and down on his cock.

My muscles tightened around him as he pushed in deeper, setting off spasms inside me as I came for him again. He fucked me post orgasm for another few minutes, thrusting upwards and pulling me down further onto his dick before reaching his goal, quietly breathing in my ear so as not to attract attention from any passers-by.

Later, I lay with my head in his lap as we sat and watched the sun set. Although he had been in my life less than a year, I couldn't imagine how empty it would feel without him.

We drove into work together Wednesday morning as Jim was going straight from work to meet Scott and I wanted to give the bookshop a deep clean before opening time.. I enjoyed sitting up front in his 4x4, recalling the fun we had in it one evening early on in our relationship. I loved to relive our sexcapades in my mind. We had such an active and imaginative sex life. Something I had never had before.

I wondered briefly if Jim's past had been full of daring public sex and naughty exotic women. But as we were just around the corner from work, it would have to be a conversation for another day.

We said goodbye outside the bookshop, kissing passionately.

'Have a good morning, beautiful,' he called after me. 'I'll see you for lunch.'

I waved goodbye and walked away from the car, giving a little bum wiggle as I went.

I stopped at the off licence on the way to dinner at Matt and Paulo's Wednesday evening feeling strangely anxious. I reached the front door and instinctively got my key out before deciding that I should knock and return the key to Matt. I no longer lived here and it was an odd feeling.

The house was silent so I knocked again, then heard footsteps on the stairs. The door flew open and there stood Paulo. I opened my mouth to speak, but the words got lost.

His dark curly hair was wet, dripping down his face. But that wasn't the reason I was suddenly mute. He had clearly just stepped out of the shower.

His chest was dark with curly hair and he was a lot more buff than he had appeared when I met him in the shop.

Unlike Jim who was practically sculpted with a small frame, Paulo was a lot beefier but still with not an inch of fat on him.

His towel – which I'm sure I used to wrap my hair in, it was so small – was tied just under his hip bones, showing the top of his pubic hair above it. An unmistakable bulge raised the towel at the front, revealing muscular thighs, also thick with dark hair.

'Ah, beleza,' he purred. 'Please come in.'

I nodded, averting my gaze as quickly as my body would allow me. I followed him through the hall and into the kitchen. 'Would you like me to put that somewhere for you?'

My eyes darted to his face, taken aback by his words.

'Excuse me?' I asked.

'The wine...should I put it in the fridge?' He grinned at my reddening cheeks.

'Oh, um, yes, that would be great, thank you,' I stammered.

He moved in close to me; I could smell his freshly washed skin. Why was he so close? I panicked. He was smiling at me and his almost-naked body was far too close to me. Close enough to pull at that towel a little, just to see what's underneath. I banished the thought as quickly as I could before I got lost in that daydream.

He put his arm around me and pulled the fridge open to put the wine in. I jumped out of the way, apologising. What an idiot! I scolded myself. I had been stood right in his way. He said nothing, but grinned at me. He clearly knew the effect he had on me and was enjoying unnerving me.

He poured two glasses of wine from another bottle in the fridge and I immediately regretted alcohol in this situation.

He stood and sipped his glass and I wished he would put some clothes on so I could regain some form of dignity and control. He didn't seem in any hurry though.

'I'm sorry... Please feel free to continue getting ready, I'm fine down here and Matt will be home soon too,' I said, trying to sound as casual as possible.

He took another sip of his wine, then put it down on the counter.

'Of course, as you wish, beleza,' he said as he crossed the kitchen.

'Paulo, what is beleza?' I asked as he walked into the hall. He turned back around and I'm sure I caught a quick glance of what he was hiding under his mini towel.

'It means beauty,' he said calmly, then turned and walked upstairs.

I was still stood frozen to the spot in the hallway a few moments later as Matt arrived home.

'Hey, Sass,' he greeted me, wrapping me into a bear hug.

'Hey you,' I said, hugging him back.

I helped him get things ready for dinner and had started to relax when Paulo came back downstairs, dressed this time thankfully.

We all talked easily and Paulo behaved himself for the remainder of the evening.

'So how are you settling in?'

'Well. Thank you. Matt has been very helpful with the area and the best places to go.'

'It must be very different to Portugal,' I said, wishing I had seen more of the world.

'Have you ever been?' he asked, as if reading my mind.

'No, I haven't,' I said.

He looked at Matt.

'I have been once,' Matt said. 'About four years ago with the guys. We stayed in Lisbon.'

'I lived a few hours from there in the north.'

We all enjoyed our food. Having stuck to just one glass of

wine at the start of the night, I was able to drive home.

I said my goodbyes in the hallway, and, after I gave Matt a big hug, I turned to Paulo, feeling awkward once more. He pulled me close to him with his hands on my hips and kissed my cheek lightly.

'Safe drive, beleza, thank you for your lovely company.' I blushed a little and thanked them both, then hurried out to my car.

Jim was still out when I arrived home and I realised it was the first time I'd ever been at the apartment on my own.

I went straight into the en suite and turned the taps on in the bath. I lit some candles and put a few drops of essential oil under the tap. Pulling off my clothes, I put my hair up into a messy bun on top of my head.

Steam filled the room with the scent of fresh orange as I stepped into the giant bathtub and laid my head against the roll top.

I breathed in the sweet scent and closed my eyes.

Paulo appeared in my mind, wrapped in his little towel. He was close to me again, just as he was when he reached for the fridge. But, this time, he wasn't reaching for anything, except me.

I imagined myself gently tugging at his towel and letting it slip to the floor, then built a picture in my mind of what his cock looked like.

I let my imagination run wild, building the perfect dick – thick and long – as I ran my fingers down my stomach and began to pleasure myself.

I remembered the shower head and how good it had felt when Jim held it against me.

Feeling momentarily guilty as Jim's image entered my

mind, I decided to push his face away for a few minutes more.

Paulo was back, forcefully pleasing me in his passionate Portuguese way.

I moved the shower head over my clit with one hand and thrust my fingers deep inside myself with the other. As I stroked my G-spot, I could almost feel his thick cock inside me, and, minutes later, my muscles were in a spasm as I came hard.

As soon as I had, I felt intensely guilty. How could I have thoughts like that about another man? Even though our extra-curricular activities as a couple were surely worse than what I had just done, this felt wrong. Rupert and Jess had seen more than my gynaecologist, but I didn't fantasise about them or have any feelings of lust for them.

I fell asleep, stirring just a little as Jim got in and rolled over, cuddling into his chest.

Chapter 23

Jim was gone when I woke Thursday morning. He had left a note to say he had a few errands to run before he opened up. I felt a little gutted that I hadn't seen him properly since Tuesday night; I was looking forward to an evening in together.

It was coming up to lunchtime and I was sorting out stock in the back when I heard the door open.

'I'll be with you in a sec,' I called out as I jotted down on my pad where I had got to, then wandered out to the shop to see Paulo's back to me as he perused the shelves.

I bit my lip and screwed my eyes up tight, hoping he would be gone when I opened them again. He was not.

'Hi, Paulo,' I said, breezily. 'What brings you in again so soon?'

'Beleza, I am looking for a new book,' he said, giving me that smile. I stood and thought for a moment, remembering the type of books we had discussed.

I walked over to one of the shelves and started telling him about an author I had recently discovered that he might like. I could feel his breath on the top of my head as he towered above me.

'I thought about you,' he said conversationally. 'I have thought about you a lot since I first met you here.'

I froze, unsure what to say. He touched my arm and I spun around, forgetting how close he was and he looked down at me, dark eyes full of promise.

'I have a boyfriend,' was all I could say as I ducked under his arm and free of him. Boyfriend sounded so immature; what Jim and I had was far more than that.

'Yes, Jim, the deli boy,' he said mockingly. That was a mistake. Anger replaced the heat between us. 'You have felt the passion too, beleza. I know you have.'

I looked away from him and busied myself at the till.

'That's beside the point,' I said, kicking myself for admitting it to him. 'I am in a serious relationship and this is inappropriate,' I said, finding my composure.

'Please forgive me, Saskia.' My name rolled off his tongue deliciously. 'I should not have said anything. I will respect your relationship and you will not hear another word about it.'

I looked up and he was stood in front of me, looking like a wounded animal.

'Thank you,' I said, feeling brave and a little disappointed. He held my gaze and I felt unable to look away as if he had some form of power over me and that he somehow knew I had masturbated to an idea of him in my mind.

As we stood in silence, the door opened and Jim walked in. I jumped away from Paulo guiltily and stumbled over introductions. Paulo grinned.

'Nice to meet you, Paulo,' Jim said, sternly shaking his hand. 'Saskia, I brought you lunch,' he said, pulling me into a tight grip and kissing me, reclaiming what belonged to him. I thanked him and led him to the counter, leaving Paulo to browse for his new book. Jim fixed me with an unhappy stare, but clearly thought better of having the conversation in front of Paulo. He made enough small talk to warrant the visit and left me to my lunch. Paulo left shortly afterwards and I spent the rest of my afternoon reprimanding myself for being so stupid and dreading the conversation that was coming later this evening. I had done nothing wrong, but my face would betray me – as it always did – and reveal the guilt of my lust.

I locked up the shop a little early and popped into the local supermarket to grab some food. I hoped that if I could make us a nice tea, it might soften the blow.

Dinner was almost ready when Jim came in through the front door. He must have been out running as he was sweaty and dressed in shorts and a vest top.

'I'm going for a shower, Sass,' he said without even looking at me.

'OK,' I said. 'Dinner will be ready in about ten minutes.'

He nodded and disappeared into the bedroom. My heart sank. He was clearly very annoyed; I didn't even get a kiss. I waited until I heard the shower turn off then gave him a few minutes to dress before serving the lasagne . He sat down at the table and started to eat without a word.

'Is everything OK?' I asked gently.

'Yeah, I'm sorry, Saskia,' he said, making eye contact for the first time since arriving home. 'This is all lovely, thank you. I'm just not feeling myself this evening.' His eyes looked red.

'Can I do anything to help?' I asked, not wanting to bring up Paulo. He finished his last mouthful and stood up.

'No, beautiful,' he said, kissing me on the head. 'You are amazing, as always. I just need to clear my head. I'm going to have a lie down if that's OK?'

I nodded.

This wasn't about Paulo then. I gave him a kiss and watched him go into the bedroom and close the door behind him.

I woke the next morning to an empty bed again. I went into the en suite and saw a note on the sink telling me that he had gone for a run. I showered and dressed and was just finishing my breakfast when he came in.

'I've asked Billy to open up this morning as I have some stuff to sort out so you go on into work, babe, and I'll see you for lunch. He gave me a kiss on the cheek and a brief hug.

I held onto him as he tried to pull away. 'Please tell me what's the matter?' I begged. 'Have I done something wrong?' He pulled me in tightly and kissed the top of my head.

'No, Saskia, you could never do anything wrong. I just have some stuff going on and I need to put it straight in my head. I love you, beautiful.'

He went into the bedroom and I heard the water turn on in the shower. Already bordering on being late for work, I reluctantly left him. We really needed to talk, but I had another book club tonight and he obviously wasn't ready to share whatever it was he was going through.

I counted down to lunchtime, having thought of little other than Jim.

As soon as it became late enough to eat again, I flipped the sign around on the door and walked around to the deli.

As I stood in line where it had all begun, I watched my love serving customers. He looked so sad, so vacant. Something was wrong and my gut was telling me that, whatever it was, it didn't mean anything good. I had never seen him so distracted.

He smiled when he noticed me, but the smile was tinged with sadness. I tried to be positive and walked to the counter with the happiest expression I could wear. Billy looked up and waved and Jim brought over my salad.

'How is your day going?' I asked, keeping my voice light.

'Ah not too bad, Saskia' he said with a little more enthusiasm than I'd heard from him for a day or two.

I reminded him that the book club was meeting tonight and he leaned over the counter and gave me a peck on the lips as he handed my lunch over. The regulars were used to this behaviour.

I took my bag of food and slowly strolled back around to the shop feeling my sense of dread growing.

I pushed my feelings down as much as I could for the book club and it actually went really well.

Everyone had enjoyed the first book. We discussed it at great length and chose the next one for our meeting in two weeks.

The general feeling was for something a little more traditional for the next read so we had gone with *Little Women*. It wouldn't have been my first choice but I wasn't really feeling up to any kind of discussion so let it go, just wanting to get home.

By the time I got home, Jim was in bed. Either asleep or faking it so I wouldn't press him to talk.

I switched off my alarm Saturday morning and was pleased to see Jim actually next to me in bed. He was sat up against the headboard watching me as I rubbed the sleep from my eyes. 'Hi, you.' I smiled, yawning.

'Morning, beautiful.' He looked over his shoulder to his

phone on the side table.

'I have to go to my parents today. My mum has had some issues in the house and my dad has been unable to resolve them. I have Billy covering the shop and will be back tomorrow evening.'

He sounded so blunt and distant as he spoke.

'Of course,' I responded. 'Do you need my help? I could see if Matt—'

'Thanks, Saskia.' He cut me off. 'I'll be fine.' He gave me a kiss then went to get ready.

I lay back on the pillow. What was going on? He was drifting away and I had no idea why.

Julia popped back into my mind and I cursed her just for living near his parents. I wondered if he had confided in her about whatever was going on.

Saturday was long and drawn out. I felt numb with worry and helplessness. I found myself wandering aimlessly around the shop, desperately trying to find something to do to take my mind off the sickening feeling in the pit of my stomach.

I had messaged Jim telling him that I loved him and was looking forward to our next evening together. The reply had been a stock message. He was just going through the motions and I wished he would speak to me about what he was going through.

I texted Beth asking if she was free Sunday. Sensing the tone, she called me. Trying to keep tears at bay over the phone,

I could do with a chat x

Her message came back almost instantly

I can be at the apartment at 10 tomorrow morning. Is that ok? X

Thank you, that would be lovely x

I text back, feeling lucky to have such good friends around me. No matter what had gone on in my life, Beth and Matt had been the constant. Always picking up the pieces and wiping away the tears.

We had done it for each other over the years and I knew there and then that even if the worst happened with Jim, I would get through it. Beth and Matt would make sure of that.

Chapter 24

Within minutes of Beth arriving at the apartment Sunday morning, the tears were in full flow.

The way Jim had been, coupled with the guilt I felt over Paulo, had really built up and I had been holding the floodgates shut.

Beth consoled me. 'I'm sure there is a good reason for the way Jim is acting. He is so smitten with you, there has to be.'

I nodded, hoping she was right.

'You certainly don't have anything to feel guilty about either. I have met Paulo, and, my, does that man have it going on.' She closed her eyes briefly and laughed when she opened them again.

I waited up for Jim Sunday evening, and, when he arrived home, I had my new negligée on for him, covered by my robe.

I had purchased full stockings and suspenders with a Basque and crotchless panties. They were black and red with lace panels. I knew that the way he reacted to this would define whether we still had hope for us or not.

I had carefully placed new logs in the fireplace and managed to get the fire going;

unsure whether it was the chill of autumn that I felt or the coldness that our relationship had brought recently.

He looked very tired and distant as he came through the door. I welcomed him with a kiss and a glass of wine. He accepted and pulled me into a tight embrace. I let him drink his glass, which didn't take long. Then I stood up and slid the robe off my shoulders, letting it drop to the floor.

He looked me up and down and shook his head. Without words he walked over to me and got to his knees. But instead of finding my clit with his tongue as he usually did, he held me with his face against my stomach. He stayed on his knees holding me tight for what felt like an eternity, as if he didn't want to let me go. I ruffled his hair and he looked up at me, his eyes red and swollen.

Then the man I loved with all my heart slowly lowered his head and passionately took his time running his tongue around my crotch, as if for the first time. Dipping his tongue in every crevice, exploring me. It was different.

His usual frenzied, wild mouth had been replaced by this slow, intimate pace.

He pushed his tongue up inside me, still taking his time to hit every spot. I came intensely and just as slowly as he intended. My legs shook as I practically convulsed as the extreme orgasm rippled through me.

He stood and lifted me into his arms, laying me on the lounge floor on the thick, shaggy rug in front of the open fire.

I watched as he took off his clothes, one item at a time; his naked body framed by the glow of the firelight. He lay between my legs and slowly penetrated me. We became one as we made love. Each thrust pulling us a little closer together.

We moaned and moulded together and I lost track of how many times I climaxed.

He couldn't seem to get enough and kept his slow, seductive pace the whole way through. When I finally felt his muscles tighten as he came inside me, he called out my name.

He no longer held his weight up, collapsing down on top of me, pushing the air out of my chest. I held him there, close to me, wishing the moment would last forever but knowing better.

I was right to dread whatever was coming. Tonight had made this more obvious than ever.

We got into bed side by side with very few words. He didn't want to talk yet and I wasn't sure I was ready to hear it anyway.

Monday evening was when it happened. When he was ready to talk. I still wasn't ready to hear it and my heart beat in my ears as well as my chest.

'Saskia, I need you to sit down.'

My mind whirled through all the reasons I would need to sit.

Had someone died? Was he dying? Was he leaving me? I had thought of little else for the past few days and I felt sick to the pit of my stomach.

I slowly stepped backwards and sat on the edge of the sofa, unable to speak.

'I need to talk to you about something,' he continued, a perplexed look on his face.

'What is it, Jim?' I stammered, finally finding my voice.

'I had an unexpected call a week ago, from someone in my past...a past that I've never told you about.'

I regretted the fact that neither of us had ever discussed our pasts. I had no idea of his or him of mine.

'I've been trying to tell you about it ever since and just haven't known how. But now I'm too far in and have made the decisions that needed making and you need to know.'

I stared at him blankly, patiently waiting to hear whatever it was, wondering if I were just to get up and run away, would I ever have to hear it.

'Six years ago, I took a year out and was travelling. I was in Australia for a good few months. I made some good friends and was dating a girl named Becki.' He looked up at me to find me staring back, unable to form words once again.

'I told her I was going to continue traveling and come home and even asked if she wanted to join me.'

His words hurt. Even though it was way before we had met, the thought of him wanting to take another women travelling with him made my stomach knot.

'She said she couldn't leave so we said our goodbyes and we didn't speak again,' he continued.

He took a deep breath. 'Until last week... She tracked me down through social media and called me.'

'What for?' I demanded. 'Why after all this time?'

'She has a rare form of leukaemia and this has made her reassess some previous decisions.'

'Like what?' I spat. 'After six years, what has that got to do with you?'

Jim looked down at his hands. 'She was pregnant when I left, Sass, she never told me. I have a five-year-old son and she wants me to get to know him in what little time she has left and eventually take full custody of him.'

I sat open-mouthed. 'I um, I...' was all I could manage.

'His name is Luka.'

I didn't want to know his name. I didn't care about the child who was taking away the love of my life.

'I need to move to Australia, at least for a while,' he finished, unloading more hurt onto me.

I stared at the wall, tears slowly creeping from the corners of my eyes.

'Please say something, Saskia,' he pleaded, his face filled with pain.

'Are you going?' I asked without looking at him.

'He's my son... I can't not.'

My world fell apart at that moment. The tears were now falling unashamedly down my cheeks.

'Will you come with me?'

I looked up at him, his beautiful face contorted with agony.

'Leave my life behind, everything I know, to travel to the other side of the world to play families with your new son and your ex?'

'I'm so sorry, Saskia. I don't know what else to do. I love you so much and I can't bear to lose you. But how could I leave a child without any parents? Her mother is in very poor health so can't take care of him. He has no one else.'

I stood up. 'I can't do this right now, Jim. This is far too much to take in.'

Jim looked down again, wringing his hands. 'My flight is booked for two weeks' time. I'm so sorry.'

Pain clouded my brain and my heart physically hurt as I turned around and walked from our apartment.

He watched me leave as the tears poured down his face. I looked back at him as I got to the top of the stairs.

The man I loved with every part of me had hurt me far more than I could ever have imagined.

If this is the real thing... I don't want it.

To be continued.........

Printed in Great Britain
by Amazon